A Novel

THE WOLF IN THE GALLERY

J. CHESTER

A Novel

THE WOLF IN THE GALLERY

J. CHESTER

For information address: J's Personal Services LLC via email.
Jarvaris Chester
jspersonalservicesllc@gmail.com
Library of Congress Cataloging -in- Publication Data has been applied for.
Paperback ISBN: 979-8-9884648-9-1

#001 Edition 2026

Fear.. it gnashes and shows its teeth.

The Wolf, it circles.

Chaos wears many faces ~ but shares one hollow hunger.

Still, I have to go.

Trusting Him fully.
Leaning on nothing seen.

Acknowledging Him in every way ~
The path, straight.

Not easy.~
Straight.

~ / an intentional pause

PROLOGUE

I feel him before I see him.

It is a cold trail down my spine. A tightening at the back of my neck. A prickling across the fine hairs of my forearms that has nothing to do with the temperature of the room and everything to do with something older than reason ~ some pre-verbal knowledge that lives below the brain, in the places the body keeps its oldest memories.

I am standing in a gallery full of chatter and clinking glasses and expensive cologne. The lighting is warm. The art is inoffensive. There is no logical reason to feel what I am feeling.

My body does not care about logic.

I don't turn around.

I learned that, years ago, long before I understood why I had learned it.

To turn is to acknowledge. To acknowledge is to invite.

So I keep my eyes on the canvas in front of me ~ a bruise of indigo and gold, something the placard calls Grief Study No. 4 ~ and I breathe. I let him look.

I let him believe I don't notice.

His cologne reaches me before his voice does. Cedar and smoke. Something warm underneath, something that has been carefully chosen to be remembered.

"A woman who actually looks at art."

He appears at my shoulder the way expensive things appear ~ without announcement, as if their arrival is simply inevitable. His voice is warm. His smile, when I finally turn, is wider than it needs to be.

His eyes are not smiling at all.

They are cataloging me. The set of my shoulders. The angle of my chin. The way my fingers have tightened, without my permission, around the stem of my wine glass. He absorbs each detail with the quiet efficiency of a man who has done this many times before, who has learned that the inventory must be completed before the approach, because you cannot dismantle something you haven't first studied.

He sees everything.

And I see, in that first moment, what exactly he is.

I used to trust my body.

Before my marriage, before eight years of being told that my instincts were a malfunction, I knew things. Not with my mind ~ with my skin. The way it would pull tight when someone's kindness was a performance. The way it would flood with wrongness in a room that looked, by every visible measure, safe.

I was taught to stop. Not cruelly ~ that is the part that takes years to understand. It was done gently. With love, or something that wore love's face. You're so sensitive. You always imagine the worst. He didn't mean it like that. You always do this ~ you take a perfectly nice moment and you find a way to make it frightening.

After enough repetitions, you learn. You learn to take the voice that says something is wrong and you press it down, firm and steady, until it stops making noise. You learn to call it anxiety, or overthinking, or the residue of a difficult childhood. You learn to be reasonable.

And then one day you are standing in a gallery with a man's eyes on the back of your neck and the voice is trying to speak and you have become so fluent in silencing it that you almost miss what it is saying.

Almost.

They tell you, afterward, that you should have known. They say it gently, the ones who mean well. Didn't you see the signs? As if seeing requires only eyes and not the freedom to believe what your eyes are showing you. As if a woman who has spent years being told her perception is broken can simply decide, one afternoon, to trust it again.

I saw him. I saw the wolf beneath the performance, the calculation behind the charm. My body transmitted the information clearly and without ambiguity. But I had been taught ~ so carefully, so lovingly taught ~ that my body was not a reliable narrator. That my fears were projections. That my instincts were just old wounds talking.

So when he extends his hand and says his name, I take it.

His fingers close around mine. His grip is precise. Not too firm, not too soft. The grip of a man who has practiced being exactly what the moment requires.

"Lucian," he says.

He says it like a key turning in a lock he has already found.

I didn't run. Of course I didn't. That's not how these stories go.

You want to believe you would be different. You want to believe you would feel the cold trail of that gaze and walk out, call a car, go home, lock your door. You want to believe you would listen to the voice.

But the voice is small. And he is standing there with his perfect smile and his cedar smoke and his eyes that have already learned the shape of you. And the world is full of people who would look at this scene and see a handsome man and a woman at an art opening and think: how lovely. What a nice story this could be.

What kind of broken woman, the voice in your head asks ~ the other voice, the one he hasn't planted yet but doesn't need to, because your ex-husband already did ~ what kind of broken woman walks away from something nice?

That woman, I know now, is the sanest one in the room.

But I was not her yet.

This is not a story about a monster.

Monsters are easy. You name them, you defeat them, you close the book.

This is a story about what it costs a woman to learn, again and again, that her instincts are not a malfunction. That her fear is not a character flaw. That the voice which says something is wrong deserves, at minimum, the courtesy of being heard before it is dismissed.

It is a story about two kinds of wolf. The one who introduces himself at gallery openings and gives you a key and tells you that you are rare. And the one who has been sitting beside you for fifteen years, calling it love.

I did not see either of them clearly enough, for far too long.

This is the story of how I learned to look.

His name, when he says it, is Lucian.

He tells me I am different. He tells me I see things other people don't. He tells me that he recognized something in me the moment I walked into the room ~ a quality he has been searching for, that he almost stopped believing existed.

I smile back.

I smile back, and the wolf smiles too, and somewhere behind us, a woman I have known since I was twenty years old watches from across the room with an expression I will not be able to name until it is much, much too late.

ACT 1

CHAPTER 1: THE RETURN

The town looked smaller than she remembered.

Or maybe she had grown in ways that had nothing to do with height.

Maya drove down Main Street, slowly, hands tight on the wheel, the back seat of her Camry packed with everything she hadn't put in storage. Three boxes. That was what eight years of marriage left, once you subtracted what was his, what was disputed, what she had simply walked away from because fighting for it would have cost more than it was worth.

The buildings had been repainted. A few new storefronts had appeared ~ a juice bar, a co-working space, a gallery she didn't recognize. But the bones were the same. The pharmacy where she bought her first lipstick at thirteen, convinced it would change something. The diner with the broken 'O' in its sign that had been broken since she was in high school. The hardware store where Lena's father used to buy tomato cages every spring, back when Lena's mother still kept her garden.

She didn't look at the gallery.

The old gallery. The one with the iron doors and the red brick facade and the windows that looked like closed eyes. She knew it was there ~ two blocks east, unmissable ~ and she kept her eyes on the road ahead with the deliberate care of someone walking past a dog they've been told not to startle.

She was not here to revisit the past. She was here because she had run out of other options. The divorce had taken the apartment, most of the furniture, and whatever version of herself she had been for eight years. What remained fit in those three boxes, a duffel bag, and the hollow ~ the empty feeling of a woman who has finally stopped making herself small.

She passed the old high school, renovated now, unrecognizable. She passed the house where Lena's parents used to live before they moved to Scottsdale. She passed the gas station, the library, the war memorial with its single bronze soldier going green at the edges.

Then her hands took her somewhere she had not decided to go.

They always took her here, even when the rest of her was trying to do something else.

Lena's parents' old house sat at the end of a quiet street three blocks from the center of town. It had a new roof. Fresh paint ~ pale gray now, when it used to be yellow. A car in the driveway that was not Lena's father's truck. The garden was gone, replaced by something tidy and geometric: low boxwoods, white gravel, no flowers.

Lena's mother had grown sunflowers. Every summer, enormous ones, taller than the fence. Lena used to cut them and bring them to school in brown paper bags, handing them out to people she liked, which was most people, because Lena liked most people. Because Lena was the kind of person who grew toward light and wanted others to do the same.

Maya pulled over. She sat with the engine running, looking at the house where she had spent so many afternoons. Looking at the place where the sunflowers used to be.

They had sold the house four years after Lena disappeared. Her mother had told her, in a phone call that lasted less than three minutes: they needed to get away. They needed somewhere that didn't hold the shape of everything they had lost. You can't blame them for wanting to move on.

Maya had blamed them.

For years she had blamed them ~ for packing Lena's room, for accepting the police's verdict, for choosing to survive instead of continuing to fight. She had blamed them the way you blame people who remind you that grief has a limit and you have already exceeded it.

Now she looked at the house with its white gravel and its absence of sunflowers and she felt something else. Something that had no clean name. Something that sat in her chest like the last note of a song held just one beat too long.

She put the car in gear. She drove away.

The cemetery was at the edge of town, on a hill above the river. Maya had not been here in fifteen years. She had come once, the week before she left for the city, to stand at the grave and make a promise she didn't know how to keep. She had kept it anyway, in her own imperfect way ~ the questions she kept asking, the file she kept adding to, the name she never let herself forget.

But she had not come back to this hill. Not once.

She found the grave at the far end, near the fence overlooking the water. The brass plaque was smaller than she remembered, or maybe she had made it larger in her mind over the years, the way grief enlarges everything it touches.

Lena Marie Sinclair
1991 – 2009
Beloved Daughter

Beloved daughter. As though that were the whole of her. As though she had not also been a painter, a terrible cook, a person who laughed too loud in movie theaters and cried at commercials for telephone companies and once, memorably, convinced Maya to climb onto the roof of the school at midnight to watch a meteor shower that turned out to be mostly clouds.

Beloved daughter. The reduction of a whole person to the role she played in someone else's story.

Maya knelt in the grass. The ground was hard beneath the soft surface. She put her hand flat on the earth and left it there.

"Hi," she said. Her voice came out smaller than she intended. "I'm back. Don't know exactly why just yet. Maybe to remember. Maybe to finally figure out what I keep almost remembering."

The river glittered in the distance. The trees moved. A bird called once and went quiet.

"I'm sorry," she said. "For all the things I didn't see when I was standing right next to them. For the year I spent asking questions and then deciding the silence meant there were no answers. For the fifteen years after that when I told myself I hadn't really stopped ~ I'd just paused, I'd just stepped back, I was just gathering strength."

She looked at the date on the plaque. 2009. Lena had been eighteen. Maya had been eighteen. They had been so young they didn't know they were young, which is the only way you can be that young.

"I'm not pausing anymore," she said. "I don't know what I'm going to find. But I'm done being someone who looks away."

She stayed until her knees ached. She brushed the grass from her dress. She looked at the plaque one more time.

"I'll come back," she said. "When I know something. I promise."

She walked to her car without looking back.

CHAPTER 2:

She drove to the rental house without looking at the gallery. She had already passed it twice ~ once on the way in, once near the cemetery ~ and both times she had kept her eyes on the road with the practiced discipline of someone who has learned that some things require working up to.

She hadn't expected to feel it so quickly.

The house was small and white, with a porch that wrapped around the front and a swing that creaked in the still air, unhurried, like it had all the time in the world. The ceiling above was that old chalky blue paint, lifting at the corners. And the gardenias ~ God, the gardenias ~ banked heavy along the railing, their smell reaching her through the car window before she'd even opened the door. She had rented it sight unseen from a landlord she'd found online, desperate for somewhere that wasn't the apartment she had shared with Mark and wasn't her mother's spare room or a hotel where she'd lay awake listening to other people's normal lives moving through the walls.

She parked in the gravel driveway.

She sat for a moment, hands on the wheel, looking at the house.

It was temporary. Just a momentary pause on the journey. That was what she told herself. She was not staying. She was regrouping ~ her therapist's word, offered with gentle authority the way therapists offer words that are true but incomplete. "You don't have to make any decisions right now. You just need to be somewhere. You just need to let yourself land."

She got out.

The air was different here. Slower, somehow. Older ~

Inside, the landlord had left basic furniture: a couch with a floral pattern that belonged to a different decade, the kind of couch that had absorbed a thousand Sunday afternoons that weren't hers, a kitchen table with mismatched chairs that somehow worked anyway, a bed with a headboard that someone had started painting white and then lost their conviction somewhere around the second coat, leaving it that particular grey that isn't quite anything. She walked through the rooms slowly, her footsteps too loud in the empty space, the old hardwood floors announcing her under every step ~ that specific creak of an unfamiliar house, the sound of a place that doesn't know you yet. A woman taking inventory of the life she had arrived with.

The rooms smelled of lemon oil and a little of dust and underneath both, something floral she couldn't name ~ as though the house had its own ideas about welcome. The windows were the old single-pane kind, wavy glass that made the outside world look like a memory of itself. She pressed her fingers to one and felt the day's heat still caught in it.

The kitchen window looked out on a backyard gone wild ~ long grass, a rose bush that had not been cut back in years, a bird bath tilted at an angle that suggested it had given up on being level. She stood at the window and looked at it, and something in her recognized it. The general air of things that had simply continued without anyone to tend them.

Then she looked beyond it, to the left, past the neighbor's fence.

Two blocks south, visible between rooftops: the iron doors of the gallery. Even from here she could see the way the afternoon light caught the hinges.

She pulled the kitchen blind down. She went to unpack her car.

Three boxes. She carried them in one at a time, the cardboard rough against her bare arms, the gravel unsteady under her feet, the afternoon heat pressing down on each trip like a hand on her shoulder. She set them in the middle of the living room floor and looked at what she had reduced herself to.

Clothes.

Books.

The photograph of her and Mel at graduation, arms around each other, faces young, certain, and yet unaware of everything that was coming. A photograph of her parents on their wedding day, smiling at something outside the frame ~ she had always wondered what. A photograph of her and Mark on their honeymoon in Portugal, which she had packed by accident and had not yet decided what to do with. She turned that one face down without thinking about it.

And the box she had packed last. The one she had almost left in the storage unit, she had stood in the metal door half-raised, arguing with herself whether or not to leave it, the smell of old cardboard and other people's abandoned things around her. She had taken it because she always took it. Because in fifteen years she had never once been able to leave it behind.

Lena's box.

She set it on the coffee table. She sat cross-legged on the floor in front of it the way she had when she was nineteen, when she had first packed it, hands flat on her knees. The cardboard was worn soft at the corners from years of being moved, the tape gone yellow, her own handwriting on the top ~ LENA ~ in the large, unguarded letters of a girl who did not yet know how much could remain uncertain. How much you could carry without it getting lighter.

She opened it.

A bracelet first. Beaded, handmade, the kind that costs three dollars and feels like a fortune because of who gave it to you. Lena had worn it every day for the last two years of her life. Maya had found it in her dresser drawer, tucked inside a pair of rolled socks, the morning after she disappeared. Which meant she had taken it off deliberately. Which meant she had been somewhere she didn't want to wear it ~ somewhere she was trying even in that small way, to keep a piece of herself safe.

A photograph. Lena at the gallery, the night she disappeared. Someone had taken it without her knowledge ~ Lena was in profile, caught between one expression and the next, her face doing something that Maya had spent fifteen years trying to name. It was not quite fear. It was not quite recognition. It was something in between, something that happened in the body before the mind has finished understanding what the body already knows.

Maya had shown this photograph to the police, twice. Both times they had looked at it, handed it back, said: she looks fine to us. Both times Maya had taken it home and looked at it for a long time, trying to see what they saw. She never could.

And then the notebook.

Lena's notebook ~ small, cloth-covered, the kind sold in tourist shops, nothing special. Maya had taken it from Lena's room the day after she disappeared and had never opened it. In fifteen years, she had never opened it. She had carried it from apartment to apartment, city to city, always in the same box, always face-down, as if the act of not looking were a form of respect, or self-protection, or both.

She opened it now.

The first pages were blank. The second, blank. She flipped forward, methodically, her heart doing something slow and loud in her chest. Blank, blank, blank, blank ~ Lena's handwriting nowhere, as if she had sat with this notebook and been unable to begin, unable to say what she needed to say, unable to find the first word.

Or as if the first word was the only one that mattered.

At the very back, on the last page, in Lena's handwriting ~ pressed so hard the letters had almost torn through the paper:

RUN

Maya sat with the notebook in her hands for a long time.

A single word. Written in the back of a notebook that otherwise contained nothing. Written with the force of someone who needed to say it and had no time, or no safety, to say anything else. A message in a bottle, or a message to herself ~ and Maya didn't know which was worse. Lena warning someone who might find this. Or Lena trying to remind herself of something she kept forgetting.

She closed the notebook. She placed it on the coffee table. She sat with her back against the couch and her hands flat on her thighs and she breathed ~ in, slowly, out slowly ~ the way her therapist had taught her, the way that felt absurd and also occasionally prevented her from disappearing entirely into herself.

Lena knew. Lena saw something, or felt something, or understood something, and she wrote that one word in the back of a notebook and she never told anyone. Or she tried to tell someone and they didn't hear her. Or someone heard her and decided it didn't mean what it meant.

Maya thought about the last time she saw Lena. The gallery opening. Lena pulling at her own sleeve, looking at the door. I need to tell you something.

Tell me now, Maya had said.

Not here. Later. I'll call you.

She never called.

Her phone buzzed. Mel.

Mel: You here yet? Wine is open. If you make me drink alone I will never forgive you !

Maya looked at the notebook on the coffee table. She looked at the box. She looked at the photograph of Lena's face caught between one moment and the next.

She almost texted: I found something. I need you to come here.

She didn't. She put the phone down. She wasn't sure why ~ only that some instinct, rusty with disuse, said: wait. Just wait.

She texted instead: Give me twenty minutes. Save me a glass.

She put Lena's notebook in her bag. She didn't examine the impulse. She just did it.

Then she got up, looked at herself in the small bathroom mirror ~ tired, older than she felt, familiar in the way that your own face is familiar even when you've spent years becoming a stranger to yourself ~ and she went to see Mel.

CHAPTER 3:

Mel's apartment was three blocks away, on the second floor of a building that still had the same cracked tile in the lobby and the same smell ~ old wood and someone else's cooking ~ that it had had when they were twenty-two. Mel had moved in at the beginning of senior year and had never left. Maya used to tease her about it. You're going to die in this apartment.

Mel always shrugged. I like it here. It knows me.

The door was ajar when Maya arrived. Music playing inside, something with a beat. And then Mel appeared in the gap, a glass in each hand, a smile so immediate and uncomplicated that Maya felt, for the first time in months, the specific relief of being somewhere she was expected.

"You look like a Victorian orphan who's been on the road too long," Mel said, handing her a glass. "When did you last eat something that grew in the ground?"

"I had a salad."

"Gas station?"

"The lettuce was real."

"The lettuce is always real, Maya, that's the trick." Mel pulled her inside and Maya let herself be pulled, because Mel had always had this quality ~ this particular gravitational field that made it easy to let her decide the direction. It was something Maya had loved about her for fifteen years. Tonight, stepping into the warm apartment with its candles and its careful arrangements, she let herself love it again without examining it. "I'm ordering pizza. The good kind. Come sit."

The apartment was the same as it had always been. Too many candles. Too many throw pillows, accumulated over years in colors that didn't quite match but somehow worked. Photographs on every surface, framed and intentional ~ the two of them at graduation, at a concert, at a beach in North Carolina the summer after they finished college. Mel curated her life with the care of someone who understood that objects held meaning and meaning had to be tended.

Maya settled into the corner of the couch. She noticed, as she always noticed, that there were no photographs of anyone else. No family, no other friends, no ex-boyfriends documented and then archived. Just the two of them, everywhere, their friendship the only relationship Mel had ever seen fit to preserve in frames.

She had always found it touching.

She found it touching now. She told herself that.

Mel dropped beside her, close, their knees almost touching, and looked at her with the focused attention she had always brought to things that mattered to her.

"Tell me," she said.

"There's not that much to tell."

"You drove four hours with everything you own in a Camry. There is always that much to tell."

Maya drank. The wine was good ~ cold and slightly sharp, the kind that tastes like someone made a decision about it. "He got the apartment. And the dog."

"The dog deserves better than him and you both know it."

"He never walked her."

"I know. You deserve better than him too, for what it's worth." Mel said it easily, matter-of-factly, the way she had always said the things Maya found hardest to say to herself. "So. You're here. What do you want?"

Maya looked at her wine. She thought about Lena's grave. The brass plaque. The word on the last page of the notebook.

"I want to figure out who I am," she said, "when no one is telling me who to be."

Mel was quiet for a moment. Then she reached over and squeezed Maya's hand. Her grip was warm, firm ~ a little longer than necessary, but Mel had always held on like that, like she wanted to make sure you felt it.

"That," she said, "is a perfect answer."

The pizza arrived. They ate it on the couch, no plates, the way they always had. Mel talked ~ about her cat's ongoing vendetta against the mailman, about her neighbor who'd moved out, about the man she was dating who was fine, perfectly fine, absolutely and completely fine.

"Fine means you're going to end it."

"I need to work up to it. I can't just drop a person."

"You have dropped every person you've dated within six weeks."

"I've gotten better at the transition." Mel pulled a string of cheese off her slice. "He's not bad. He's just... predictable. He orders the same thing every time we go out. I find that exhausting."

"Some people would find that comforting."

"Some people," Mel said, "are wrong."

They laughed. It was easy, the way it had always been easy, the frequency of it unchanged after all the years and distance. Maya let herself settle into it. The wine. The bad pizza. The candlelight. The simple, uncomplicated fact of Mel across from her, exactly as she had always been.

Then Mel said: "You went past the gallery."

It wasn't a question. Maya looked up.

"I drove past it," she said carefully. "I didn't stop."

"I know." Mel's voice was even. Gentle. "I just want you to know ~ it's different now. New owner. New art. It's not the same place it was."

"I know it isn't."

Maya waited for the obvious question. The human question ~ why did you go past it? What were you looking for? How did it feel? The question anyone who didn't already know the answer would have asked.

Mel didn't ask it. She reached for her wine instead, easy and unhurried, as if the going past were already accounted for. As if it required no explanation because the explanation was already understood.

I know, she had said. Not I figured or I wondered.

I know.

Maya held the thought for a moment. Then she set it down, gently, the way you set down something fragile you've decided not to examine yet. Mel had known her for fifteen years. Of course she anticipated her. That was what it meant to be known by someone that long ~ the anticipation wasn't eerie, it was intimacy. It was love.

She almost believed it.

"And you don't have to go anywhere near it," Mel continued. "You don't have to do anything you're not ready for." She set her plate down and turned slightly, tucking one leg under herself ~ the posture she adopted when she was going to say something she'd thought about. "You're allowed to just be here, Maya. You don't have to make this about Lena right away. You don't have to investigate anything. You're allowed to just come home."

Maya looked at her. The candlelight made Mel's face soft, familiar. This was the voice she had been hearing since she was twenty years old ~ steady and warm and certain in the way that certain people are certain, not because they have all the answers but because their certainty itself is a kind of shelter.

"I know," Maya said.

But she thought: she didn't ask me why I went past it. She just knew. And now she's telling me not to look.

She didn't let herself hold the thought. She finished her wine. She let Mel refill it.

It was late when she finally stood to leave. Mel walked her to the door and wrapped her in a hug that smelled like wine and the particular candle she'd been burning for years, cedar and something sweet. Cedar. Maya noticed it distantly, without knowing why she noticed it, the way you notice something your body has filed before your mind catches up.

"You're going to be okay," Mel said, her face against Maya's hair. Her arms tightened just a fraction ~ that familiar holding on, that little more than necessary. "You're back. You're here." She pulled back and looked at Maya's face with an expression that was ~

What was it?

Warm, certainly. Relieved. But something else underneath, something that moved through her eyes too quickly to name before it was gone, replaced by the familiar smile. Not quite relief, Maya thought. Something more like ~ satisfaction. The quiet, private satisfaction of someone whose plan is proceeding as expected.

She decided she was tired. She decided she was reading things into a face she had known for fifteen years. She decided that exhaustion and grief and the accumulated strangeness of being back in this town were making her see edges where there were none.

She was good at deciding things. She had been doing it for years.

"Sleep," Mel said. "Everything is better with sleep."

"Ask me again in a month," Maya said.

"I will. I absolutely will."

Maya drove home through empty streets. The town was quiet at this hour, the kind of quiet that feels like a held breath. She passed the pharmacy, the diner, and then ~ she was not going to look but she looked anyway ~ *The Gallery*.

She stopped the car.

The gallery was dark. The iron doors were closed. The windows were black and gave nothing back. She sat with her hands on the wheel and looked at the place where she had last seen Lena's face in profile, caught between one expression and the next.

The building looked smaller than she remembered, the way the whole town did. As if memory had been inflating things for years, trying to hold their importance, and the actual objects had quietly continued at their normal size.

She sat for a long time.

Her phone buzzed.

Unknown: Welcome home.

She stared at it. The number was not in her contacts. The area code was local. She read it three times, as if repetition would produce context.

Small town, she told herself. Word gets around. Probably someone she knew once. Probably harmless.

She almost texted back to ask who it was.

She didn't. She deleted the message. She drove home.

In the rental house, she took out her journal and opened to the first blank page. She wrote:

I'm back. I don't know exactly why. Something keeps pulling me here and I've spent fifteen years resisting it and I'm tired of resisting. I went to her grave. I opened the notebook.

She paused. Then:

RUN. She wrote it and she never told me. Or she tried to tell me and I didn't hear. I keep trying to decide which is worse and I can't.

She paused again, longer this time. Then:

Mel smells like cedar. She always has. I don't know why I'm writing that down.

I don't know why I noticed.

She closed the journal. She lay in the dark with her hand flat on the cover and listened to the house settle around her.

She didn't sleep well. She dreamt of iron doors and a girl standing in shadow, and when the girl turned, she had Lena's face and Lena's expression ~ that thing between fear and recognition ~ and she opened her mouth and said something Maya couldn't hear.

When she woke, she could not remember what it was. But her body remembered.

Her body was already afraid.

CHAPTER 4:

Maya woke to unfamiliar light.

Too low a ceiling. Too many windows. A silence that was not the silence of her old apartment ~ no traffic, no one in the hallway, no radiator clicking through the wall ~ but something older and more complete, the silence of a small town at dawn that has not yet remembered to make noise.

She lay still, her hand still on her journal, her body heavy in the particular way that follows exhaustion without rest. The dream was already dissolving. Iron doors. A girl. Something she couldn't hear.

She got up. She made coffee. She stood at the kitchen counter with the mug between her palms and looked at the pulled-down blind over the kitchen window and thought about not lifting it.

She lifted it.

The gallery's iron doors caught the early light, two blocks south. Closed. Ordinary. Just a building.

She drank her coffee looking at it. She was trying to establish a relationship with it that was professional rather than haunted. A building. Brick and iron. A place where things happened fifteen years ago that have not stopped mattering.

Her phone buzzed.

Mel: How did you sleep? Lunch? There's a place. You'll hate it. It'll be perfect.

Maya smiled. She typed back: Give me an hour.

She went to shower, and as she stood under the water, she thought about the text from last night. Welcome home. She had told herself it was nothing. She still told herself it was nothing. But her body, which had been trying to tell her things for years and had lately been getting better at being heard, catalogued it differently.

She noted that she had deleted it before she could show it to anyone.

She noted that she didn't know why.

CHAPTER 5:

The diner was the kind of place that had not updated its menu since 1987 and had made peace with this fact. Vinyl booths, cracked at the seams. Fluorescent lights that made everyone look slightly unwell. A laminated menu that had been laminated over the original lamination at some point, producing a surface of such deep yellow it was almost amber.

Mel was already there, corner booth, back to the wall, coffee in hand. She waved when Maya walked in with the enthusiasm of someone who has been looking forward to exactly this. Maya slid in across from her and picked up the menu and then set it down because the menu was not going to change no matter how long she looked at it.

"Told you," Mel said. "You hate it."

"It's aggressively itself."

"The pancakes are criminally bad. You'll love them."

They ordered. The pancakes were, in fact, terrible ~ dense and slightly sweet in a way that suggested the batter had been made in quantity and refrigerated long enough to develop opinions. Maya ate three.

They talked easily. Mel was good at this ~ at sustaining conversation the way you sustain a fire, adding the right thing at the right moment to keep it going. She told stories about the town: who had moved, who had opened a business, who was having an affair that everyone knew about except apparently the people most relevant to it. Maya listened, laughed, let herself be carried by the rhythm of it.

She was halfway through her coffee when she noticed it.

Not anything Mel did. Nothing she could point to directly. Just a quality in what Mel was saying ~ a pattern that Maya's mind, trained by years of marriage to a man who chose his words like chess moves, kept snagging on.

About the gallery: "You should go, actually. Not for the Lena stuff ~ just to go. It's completely different now. New owner, new shows, no reason for it to feel like anything other than a gallery." Said lightly. Said as though it had occurred to her just now.

About Lena's parents: "They did what they had to do. You know? You can't maintain that kind of grief indefinitely. At some point you have to let yourself live." Said warmly. Said with compassion. Said as a kind of permission.

About the night Lena disappeared: "You did everything right, Maya. You waited for her. You called. You reported it. You were eighteen. You were not equipped to do more than that and you have to let yourself off the hook."

All of it reasonable. All of it kind. All of it pointing, gently and consistently, in the same direction: away from looking closer.

Maya made herself notice this and then made herself release it. Mel had been saying these things, in various forms, for fifteen years. They were not new. They were comfort, not conspiracy. She was tired and looking for patterns and she should not mistake care for something darker just because she had spent too long in a marriage where care was a performance.

"Can I ask you something?" Maya said.

"Always."

"The night Lena disappeared. You left the gallery early ~ you've always said that. Around nine."

Mel nodded. Something happened in her hands ~ a stillness, too deliberate, the stillness of someone who has heard a question before and has the answer ready and is being careful about how ready it sounds. Her coffee cup stayed exactly where it was, both palms flat on the table on either side of it, like a person bracing a surface that isn't moving.

"I had an early class the next morning. You know this."

"I know. I just ~ I've been thinking about it. Whether there was anything else. Anything you remember now that maybe didn't seem important then."

Mel looked at her steadily. Her hands were flat on the table. "I've told you everything I remember, Maya. Many times."

"I know you have. I'm sorry. I'm just ~ being back here makes it feel close again."

"I understand." Mel's voice was soft. She reached across the table and covered Maya's hand with hers. "That's completely natural. But you can't solve it by going over it again. You've been over it thousands of times. If there were something to find in what we already know, you'd have found it."

Maya looked at Mel's hand on hers. Warm. Familiar. The hand of a woman who had held hers through everything.

She nodded. She smiled. She ordered more coffee.

She did not say: you moved your hands before I finished asking the question. She did not say: you knew what I was going to ask before I asked it, and you were already holding yourself very still, and I noticed.

She did not say any of it.

But when the check came and Mel reached for it ~ insisting, the way she always insisted, the way she had always been the one who paid and decided and managed the practical details of their friendship ~ Maya watched her hands again. Steady now. Relaxed. The stillness gone, replaced by the easy competence of a woman entirely in control of her environment.

Two different pairs of hands, Maya thought. One for when she's listening. One for when she's been asked something.

She filed it away without examining it. She had been doing that a lot since she came back. Building a drawer of things she wasn't ready to open.

Outside, the afternoon had gone gold and soft. They stood on the sidewalk in the particular way of two people who have been talking for two hours and are not quite ready to stop.

"Come for dinner Thursday," Mel said. "I'll cook. Something that actually grows from the ground."

"I'll bring wine."

"Bring the good kind. You know what I like."

Maya did know. She had known for fifteen years. She knew Mel's wine and her candle and the particular throw pillow she always reached for when she was settling in for a long conversation. She knew the sound of her laugh and the register her voice dropped to when she was being serious and the way she tilted her head when she was deciding something.

She had always called this intimacy.

Walking home, she turned it over quietly. Intimacy meant knowing someone. It meant the accumulation of years producing a map of a person ~ their habits, their preferences, their tells.

Their tells.

She stopped walking.

Mel knew her tells too. Every one of them. Fifteen years of watching Maya think and feel and react, fifteen years of being the person Maya called first, told first, trusted with the unedited version of everything.

Mel had her map. The whole of it. Every place she was weak, every wound, every door that opened if you pressed it the right way.

She stood on the sidewalk in the gold afternoon and she thought about that for a long time.

Then she thought about a man at a gallery opening who had told her: I could see the exact shape of a person's self-doubt. It was like a topographical map.

She thought about how quickly Lucian had known where to press.

She thought about who could have told him where to look.

She walked home. She did not run.

That night she opened her journal. She wrote down everything Mel had said about the gallery, about Lena's parents, about that night. She wrote it in a list. She read it back.

Then she wrote:

Why does every version of this conversation end with me being told to look somewhere other than where I'm looking?

She stared at that for a long time. Then, below it, smaller:

She knew what I was going to ask before I asked it. Her hands went still. I noticed and I didn't say anything and I don't know if that was wisdom or cowardice.

Lucian said he could read a person's self-doubt like a map. He found mine so quickly. He knew exactly where I was weak before I'd told him enough to know.

I told Mel everything. For fifteen years I told her everything.

I'm going to sit with that and not decide what it means yet. I'm going to be fair. I'm going to be careful.

But I'm writing it down. Because I have learned, the hard way, that the things you don't write down are the things that later get rewritten for you.

She closed the journal. She put it under her mattress.

Not on the nightstand. Under the mattress.

She wasn't ready to examine why that felt necessary.

But her body, which had been trying to tell her things for years and was getting better at being heard, had already decided.

CHAPTER 6:

She was waiting for something, though she couldn't have said what. For the right moment. For something to tell her that she was doing this for the right reasons and not just because she had nowhere else to put her grief. For the courage to walk through an iron door she had been avoiding for fifteen years.

On the third evening, her phone buzzed. An unknown number ~ a different one from the welcome home text, though the area code was the same.

Unknown: I knew Lena. I know what happened to her. If you want the truth, meet me at the gallery. Tomorrow. 8 PM. Come alone.

Maya sat with her phone for a long time.

She thought about calling Mel. She picked up her phone to do it. She thought about Mel's hand on hers at the diner. The way she said you've been over it thousands of times. The way she said look somewhere other than where you're looking.

She put the phone down.

She wrote back: I'll be there.

Then she sat in the quiet of her rental house, the gallery two blocks south, Lena's notebook in her bag, and she tried to name what she was feeling.

Not fear. Or not only fear. Something else underneath it ~ something that felt, uncomfortably, like recognition. Like a door that has been locked for a very long time is finally being tried from the other side.

CHAPTER 7:

She walked. Two blocks. The same streets she had walked at eighteen, going to gallery openings with Lena, going to gallery openings without Lena, going to the gallery after Lena disappeared to ask questions that no one would answer.

The same iron doors. Closed. The windows dark. Eight-fourteen PM.

She had arrived early on purpose. She stood across the street, half in shadow, and looked at the building. Allowing herself, for once, to feel what she actually felt rather than managing it.

She felt afraid. She felt ready. She was not sure these were different things.

At eight exactly, the door opened.

A man stood in the threshold. Tall, dark-haired, wearing a jacket that had seen better decades. His face was not handsome in the way that announces itself ~ it was the kind of face that accrued, that you looked at longer and longer because something kept emerging from it. A scar along his jaw, old and faded. Lines around his eyes that spoke of a person who had spent a lot of time looking carefully at things that were difficult to look at.

He was perhaps forty. He looked at Maya across the street with an expression she recognized: the recognition of someone you've been waiting for.

"Maya," he said. His voice carried easily in the quiet street. "I was starting to think you wouldn't come."

She crossed. She stopped three feet away, out of arm's reach. Old instinct. "Who are you?"

He stepped forward, into the light spilling from the open door. He held his hands slightly away from his body ~ an old gesture, she thought, the gesture of someone who had learned that showing your hands mattered.

"My name is Daniel Sinclair," he said. "I was Lena's brother."

Maya looked at him. His eyes were dark brown, and they were, she noticed, exactly the same color as Lena's.

"She never mentioned a brother," Maya said.

"I know." He stepped back, gesturing into the gallery. "Come in. I'll explain."

Every instinct she had been practicing said: Assess. She assessed. He was not blocking her exit. He was not moving toward her. His hands were visible. The street behind her was open. She had her phone.

She went in.

CHAPTER 8:

The gallery had changed. New white walls, new lighting, new art in new configurations. But the floor was the same ~ wide-plank wood that creaked in the same places it had always creaked ~ and the smell was the same, something like linseed and age and the particular dust of a room where people try to make beautiful things.

Maya stopped in the center of the main room. She stood where she had stood fifteen years ago, waiting for Lena, watching the crowd, holding a glass of wine she didn't want. She turned slowly, letting the space settle around her. Here: where she had last seen Lena's face. There: where she had first noticed a man watching her from across the room. Somewhere between the two: the moment she had decided to stop being afraid of what she might find and start looking for it instead.

She had been so young.

"Different mothers," Daniel said, from behind her. "Our father wasn't someone who stayed. Lena grew up here with her mother. I grew up in the city with mine. We knew about each other ~ letters, some visits when we were young. But by the time we were teenagers it had become easier not to make the effort." He paused. "I regret that. I've regretted it for a long time."

"Why are you here now?"

"Because he's here. And because you're here. And because those two things together are not a coincidence."

He led her to the back office. She followed.

CHAPTER 9:

The office was small and deliberately ordinary ~ a desk, a laptop, filing boxes ~ except for the wall.

Maya stood in front of it for a long time without speaking.

The wall was covered in photographs, and in the photographs was a map of fifteen years. Lena at the gallery, this gallery, the night she disappeared ~ several shots, from different angles, none of them posed. Lena on the street. Lena at a café. Lena at the edge of a crowd, her face turned slightly away, the posture of someone who has recently noticed they're being watched.

And interspersed among the photographs of Lena: photographs of a man.

Leaving a restaurant. Standing outside a building Maya didn't recognize. Getting into a car. In one photograph ~ clearer than the others, taken from a distance but with a good lens ~ his face turned directly toward the camera, as if he knew it was there. As if he was allowing it.

He was perhaps forty-five in the recent photos. Dark hair, some silver at the temples. The kind of face that expensive things sometimes produce: symmetrical, controlled, maintained. His eyes were light ~ gray or pale blue, impossible to tell from the photographs ~ and even at this remove, even in a grainy image on a crowded wall, there was something in them that made Maya's skin register something before her mind did.

She knew that quality. She had experienced it, standing in front of a bruise-colored painting, before a man materialized at her shoulder and said a woman who actually looks at art.

"Who is he?" she asked.

Daniel came to stand beside her. "His name is Lucian Voss. He was an architectural intern fifteen years ago ~ he was doing a residency here, working on a renovation project in the old warehouse district. He attended this gallery's openings regularly. He was here the night Lena disappeared." He paused. "He was the last person seen speaking to her."

Maya turned to look at him. "You think he did something to her."

"I know he did something to her." Daniel's voice was flat and factual, the voice of someone who has moved past the question of whether and arrived at the much harder work of how and why and what now. "I've spent fifteen years building a case that no one will take seriously enough to act on. But I've found things. And I've found other women."

"What other women?"

He turned from the wall and went to his desk. He pulled a thick file from the bottom drawer and held it out.

"Sit down," he said. "This is going to take a while."

CHAPTER 10:

He spread the file across the desk. Photographs, printouts, handwritten notes in a small precise script ~ the accumulation of a man who has been looking carefully at something for a very long time.

"His pattern goes back at least fifteen years, possibly further," Daniel said. "He targets women who are in transition. Rebuilding from something ~ a divorce, a loss, an illness, anything that has left them doubting themselves. He finds them in galleries, or at the kinds of events galleries host. He's charming. He pays attention in a way that feels rare because, for most of them, it is rare ~ they've spent months or years being told their perceptions are wrong, and here is a man who seems to see them clearly."

"He tells them they're different," Maya said. "Rare."

Daniel looked at her. "He's already found you."

It wasn't a question. Maya's hands were cold. "At a gallery opening. In the city, six months ago. I ended it."

"How?"

"I saw his face when he didn't know I was watching." She looked at the photographs on the wall. "The mask came off. I saw what was underneath."

Daniel was quiet for a moment. Then: "Most women don't get that."

He pulled a photograph from the file. A young woman, dark hair, bright eyes ~ the photograph of someone who was, in that moment, happy. "Isabelle March. She was a gallery curator. She met Lucian at an opening five years ago. He told her she was the only person in the room who was actually seeing." He set the photograph down. "She's dead. The police ruled it suicide."

Another photograph. A woman with blonde hair and a smile that hadn't quite settled. "Sarah Chen. Same pattern. She got out. She's living with her sister in the suburbs and she still checks her locks four times before she sleeps."

He kept going. Photograph after photograph. Women Maya didn't know, women whose faces she would not forget. He told her what he knew about each of them in the same quiet, factual voice ~ dates, locations, the stages of the pattern, how it ended.

"Six women that I've confirmed," he said, when he stopped. "Likely more I haven't found yet. He's careful. He doesn't rush. He gives you enough time to become dependent before he starts to dismantle you, and by the time the dismantling starts you've already lost the habit of trusting your own perception."

Maya looked at the women's faces arranged across the desk. She thought about standing in front of a bruise-colored painting. She thought about a hand on her face and a voice saying you're not crazy, Maya. I would never do that to you.

"He's here," she said. "He came back."

"He comes back every few years. He has a warehouse ~ a renovation project that's been 'in progress' for fifteen years. I think it serves a purpose for him. A place he controls. A place no one else goes." Daniel's voice didn't waver. "When I heard you'd come back to town, I knew it was time. He's been watching you, Maya. I think he's been watching you for a long time."

"Since Lena."

"Since Lena." He pulled one final photograph from the file. Lena at the gallery, the night she disappeared. Her face in profile, caught between expressions. And in the background, barely in frame: a girl of eighteen, dark hair, watching.

Maya.

"You were there," Daniel said. "You saw something, even if you don't remember seeing it. He knows that. And he's been waiting for you to come back to it."

Maya stared at her own young face in the background of a photograph she had looked at a hundred times and never seen herself in.

"Show me the rest of the file," she said.

CHAPTER 11:

She left the gallery at half past midnight. The file was in her bag ~ copies Daniel had made, organized into a folder with tabs. Her head was full of names and dates and the faces of women she had never met who had all been told, at some point, by a man with pale eyes, that they were rare.

She walked home through empty streets. She was not looking at anything. She was seeing something else: a wall of photographs, a pattern extending backward through fifteen years, a man who had been in her peripheral vision since she was eighteen and who she had never clearly seen.

She was half a block from home when her phone buzzed.

Mel: How was your evening? You went quiet. Everything okay?

Maya stopped walking. She looked at the message. Then she typed:

Maya: Do you know someone named Daniel Sinclair?

The response took longer than Mel's responses usually took.

Mel: Come over. We need to talk.

Maya stood on the empty street for a moment. The gallery was behind her, two blocks north. The rental house was ahead. Mel's apartment was to the left.

She stood at the center of these three points and felt the particular stillness of a moment before something changes.

Then she turned left.

CHAPTER 12:

Mel's apartment was warm. The same candles, the same music, the same throw pillows arranged with the precision of someone who has done it so many times it has become automatic. But something was different tonight. Something in the quality of the warmth, as if it were slightly too deliberate ~ a stage set for a particular scene rather than a room someone actually lived in. Maya noticed this and then noticed herself noticing it and told herself she was tired and looking for things that weren't there.

She was getting better at catching herself doing that. She wasn't sure yet whether that was progress or its own kind of problem.

Mel was sitting on the couch when Maya arrived, not curled up in her usual way but upright, a glass of wine held in both hands. Her face was pale. Maya had not seen Mel's hands shake before. They were shaking now ~ just slightly, just enough to be visible if you were looking, and Maya was looking, because Maya had learned that the hands told the truth before the voice did.

"You saw him," Mel said. It was not a question.

"I saw Daniel Sinclair. Lena's half-brother." Maya sat in the chair across from her. She did not take off her coat. "You knew him."

"I knew of him. He came to me, years ago ~ three or four years after Lena disappeared. He'd been asking questions around town. He said he had evidence of a pattern, of other women, of a man named Lucian Voss." Mel looked at her glass. "He asked if I knew anything. About Lena. About that night."

"What did you tell him?"

"I told him I'd left early. I told him I didn't see anything." She paused. The pause had the quality of something rehearsed ~ not long enough to be suspicious, not short enough to be natural. The pause of a woman who has told this story before and knows exactly where the pause belongs. "That wasn't entirely true."

Maya went very still. "Tell me what you saw."

Mel set her glass down. She pressed her hands together in her lap as if she were cold. When she spoke, her voice was smaller ~ not the voice Maya was used to, the one that occupied space confidently, but something underneath it. Something that had been waiting.

"I was going to leave. I had my coat. I was saying goodbye to someone near the door." She stopped. "I don't remember who. Someone. A girl from one of my classes, maybe."

Maya noted this. The someone near the door, the girl from one of my classes ~ the vagueness of it. Mel remembered everything. She had always remembered everything ~ dates, names, the specific details of conversations from years ago retrieved with the accuracy of someone who had been paying close attention. The vagueness was not Mel. The vagueness was a choice.

"And I looked back into the room," Mel continued. "Just looked back, just for a moment. And I saw Lena."

"Where?"

Mel's hands tightened slightly in her lap. "Near the back. By the second doorway ~ the one that led to the office corridor."

Maya looked at her. The second doorway. The one that led to the office corridor. Not near the bar or near the entrance or somewhere approximate. The second doorway. The office corridor. Specific in the way that only someone who had been close enough to see it clearly could be specific ~ not the vagueness of a glance across a crowded room but the precision of someone who had been standing nearby.

She didn't say this. She filed it.

"She was with a man," Mel said. "Older. He was standing too close. He had his hand on her arm ~ his left hand, just above her elbow." Another specific detail, arriving without effort, without the searching quality of genuine memory being retrieved. "And she was trying to move away from him. Subtly ~ you know how Lena was, she wouldn't make a scene, she was always trying not to make a scene. But she was trying to create distance and he wasn't allowing it."

"And?"

"And I left." The words came out simply, without defense. "I was eighteen. I didn't know what I was looking at. I told myself it was nothing. I told myself~"

"Mel."

"I was scared." She looked up. Her eyes were wet. "I was scared and I was eighteen and I didn't know what to do, and by the time I'd gotten outside and thought maybe I should go back in she was ~ he was ~ I went back in and I couldn't find her. She was already gone."

Maya sat with this. She sat with it for a long time, in the warm room with its careful candles and its accumulated photographs of the two of them ~ their whole friendship, curated and arranged on every surface.

She thought: she knows which hand. She knows which doorway. She knows exactly where Lena was standing.

She thought: a person who glances back across a crowded room and sees something in passing does not know which hand.

She thought: I am going to be fair. I am going to be careful. I am not going to decide what this means yet.

"Why didn't you tell me?" she asked, finally.

"Because I thought she'd turn up. Because I thought it was nothing. Because~" Mel's voice broke, just slightly, the first fracture in a voice that had always been steady. The fracture was real, Maya thought. Whatever Mel was feeling in this moment, the fracture was real. She held onto that. "Because I was afraid that if I told you, you wouldn't stop looking. And I couldn't watch you destroy yourself looking for something you might not find."

Maya looked at her. Mel's eyes were wet. Her hands were still shaking ~ still, after everything, still shaking. Whatever was beneath this confession, the shaking was real. The love was real. Maya had to hold onto that too, the way you hold onto something solid when the ground is uncertain.

"You've been carrying this for fifteen years," Maya said.

"Yes."

"And when Daniel came to you~"

"I told him the same thing I'm telling you. That I saw a man with his hand on her arm and she was trying to move away." Mel finally picked up her glass. Her hands steadied around it ~ that same quality Maya had noticed at the diner, the transition from one pair of hands to another. "That's all I knew."

It was not all she knew. Maya understood this with a certainty that sat below language, in the place the body kept its oldest knowledge. It was not all she knew. But it was, perhaps, all she was going to say tonight. And pushing further, right now, in this room, with this version of Mel ~ the pale, shaking, fractured version ~ would only close the door.

Maya had learned something from Lucian, from the long careful weeks of him. She had learned that the most important information came not when you pushed but when you waited. When you created the conditions in which a person believed they were safe.

She would wait.

"But you still didn't tell me," Maya said. Her voice was gentle. She kept it gentle.

The silence that followed was the loudest silence Maya had heard in years.

"I was trying to protect you," Mel said. "If you knew, you would go after him. You would walk into his world without enough to stop him, and he would~" She stopped. "I couldn't lose you too."

Too. The word landed and Maya let it land without touching it. Too. As if Lena were already a loss Mel had processed and filed. As if the grief of it were past tense in a way that eighteen years of genuine friendship suggested it shouldn't be.

She looked at her oldest friend. At the face she had known for fifteen years. At the hands, steadying now around the wine glass. At the photographs arranged on every surface ~ the two of them, everywhere, their friendship documented with the care of something precious and, Maya now understood, deliberately bounded. No one else. Just them. Always just them.

She thought: she loves me. That is true. Whatever else is true, that is also true. I have to hold both.

"I'm not looking for your permission," Maya said. "I want you to understand that. I'm not telling you my plan. I'm not asking you to come with me. I'm just ~ I need you to know that I am going to keep looking. Whether or not you think it's safe."

Mel looked at her. Something moved through her eyes ~ the same thing Maya had seen at the door on the first night, too fast to hold. Not fear. Something more considered. The movement of a mind behind the eyes, assessing, calculating, deciding.

"I know," Mel said. "I've always known I couldn't stop you. I was just hoping I could slow you down."

It sounded like an admission of defeat. It sounded like love.

It sounded, Maya thought, standing to leave, like someone who had been trying to manage the timing of something.

She hugged Mel at the door. Mel's arms came around her ~ tight, that little more than necessary, that familiar holding on. And there it was again. Cedar and something sweet. The candle, Maya told herself. Just the candle.

But she thought about cedar and smoke. She thought about a man at a gallery opening, materializing at her shoulder as if his arrival were inevitable.

She thought: why do they smell the same.

She didn't let herself finish the thought. She stepped back. She said goodnight. She walked down the stairs and out into the cool air and she breathed.

In the rental house, she took out her journal ~ from under the mattress, where she had put it, where it lived now. She opened it. She wrote:

She knew which hand. She knew which doorway. A person who glances back across a crowded room does not know which hand.

She said she couldn't lose me too. Too. Past tense. Lena already filed under loss.

She smells like cedar. She has always smelled like cedar. I have never thought about this before.

I am going to be fair. I am going to be careful. I am not going to decide what it means.

But I am writing it down. Because that is what I do now. I write things down so they cannot be taken from me later.

I write things down so I cannot be convinced I didn't see them.

She closed the journal. She lay in the dark.

She thought about two pairs of hands. The ones that shook and the ones that steadied. The ones that held her and the ones that went flat on a table when a question arrived they already knew the answer to.

She thought about which pair was the real one.

She didn't know yet. She was trying to be fair.

But her body, which had been trying to tell her things for years and was getting better, finally, at being heard ~ her body had already decided.

CHAPTER 13:

She went home. She made tea she didn't drink. She sat at the kitchen table with Daniel's file open in front of her and Lucian Voss's face staring up from the photographs.

She studied him the way she had learned to study things ~ without rushing toward a conclusion, letting the details accumulate. His face in different photographs, different years. The way he stood. The way he looked at the camera in the one shot where he'd known it was there: not alarmed, not evasive. Composed. As if being seen was something he had decided to allow.

A man who knows how to choose what you see.

She thought about Lena. About the last conversation, the pull at her sleeve, the I need to tell you something that became not here, later, I'll call you. She thought about the notebook and the single word at the back, pressed hard enough to nearly tear through.

She thought about Mel. About fifteen years of conversations that all, in retrospect, pointed the same direction. About the thing that had moved through Mel's eyes twice tonight, too fast to catch, like something briefly surfacing and then deliberately sinking back down.

She opened her journal. She wrote:

His name is Lucian Voss. He's been doing this for at least fifteen years. He's here now and he knows I'm here and he's waiting to see what I do next.

She paused. Then:

Mel knew. She saw something that night and she didn't tell me. She says she was protecting me. I believe she believes that. I don't know if that's the whole truth.

She closed the journal. She turned off the kitchen light. She sat in the dark for a long time.

In the dark, she felt something she had been trying to locate for fifteen years ~ something that had been buried under grief and doubt and the accumulated weight of being told her perception was broken.

It was the feeling of seeing clearly.

Not certainty. She did not have certainty yet. But clarity: the sense of the shape of a thing, even before all its edges were visible.

She was not crazy. She had never been crazy. Something had happened to Lena, and someone had done it, and the people around her ~ some of them, for reasons she did not yet fully understand ~ had been, in various ways, looking the other way.

She was not going to look the other way.

She got up. She went to bed. She left the kitchen light off.

In the morning, she would begin.

~ End of Act 1 ~

❖

ACT 2

CHAPTER 14: THE GALLERY

He is like a wolf ~ I feel his eyes before I locate them, the way you feel weather before you see sky.

The gallery is warm and crowded and full of people performing the act of looking at art. I am not performing. Or I am, but a different performance ~ the woman who came here alone to prove she could, the woman who stood in front of her bathroom mirror and said you're fine, you like art, go, the woman who is still, six weeks after signing her divorce papers, trying to locate the self that existed before eight years of being told that self was the problem.

I am standing in front of a canvas the color of a bruise. The placard calls it Grief Study No. 4. I have been looking at it for ten minutes because it is the only honest thing in the room and because it is easier than joining a conversation cluster and performing the smile.

And then: the cold.

It starts at the back of my neck. Travels down my spine in a slow, deliberate wave, like a finger tracing something. My arms prickle beneath my sleeves. My fingers tighten, without my permission, around the stem of my wine glass.

Someone is watching me. Not the way people glance at strangers in galleries. Not the way men look at women they find attractive. Something older than that. Something that has intent.

Don't turn around, says the voice I spent eight years unlearning and the last six weeks trying to recover. Turning is acknowledging. Acknowledging is inviting. Wait. Let him think you don't know.

I wait.

He is patient too. The gaze doesn't waver. It rests on me like a hand placed flat on a table ~ present, deliberate, making no pretense of accident.

Turn around, says a different part of me, older and quieter. See what you already know.

I turn.

He is standing twenty feet away, half in shadow, a glass of red wine held loose in his fingers. He is handsome in the way that certain things are handsome ~ not beautiful, not striking, but deliberate. Everything about him has been chosen. The suit that fits him too well to be off the rack. The way he stands, weight distributed, occupying space without appearing to try. The hair, the jaw, the three days of stubble that says I could shave but I have decided this is better.

His eyes are light. Gray or pale blue ~ I cannot tell from here. But I can see that they are not doing what his face is doing. His face is doing something warm, something that might be the beginning of a smile. His eyes are doing something else entirely.

They are cataloging me.

The set of my shoulders. The tilt of my chin. The way my fingers have tightened around my glass, which he has noticed, which he filed away the moment it happened. He is not looking at me the way a person looks at someone they find interesting. He is looking at me the way a person looks at something they are deciding about.

Most people, caught staring, look away. He doesn't. He holds my gaze across the crowded room and his mouth curves slowly ~ not a smile exactly, more the shape a mouth makes when something has confirmed what it already expected ~ and then he moves.

He doesn't hurry. The crowd parts for him without appearing to notice it's doing so. He walks the way people walk when they have never doubted their right to move through a space.

He stops at my shoulder. Close enough that I can smell him before he speaks.

Cedar and smoke. Something warmer underneath ~ something that has been selected to be remembered.

"A woman who actually looks at art," he says. His voice is warm, low, the kind of voice that sounds like it's smiling even when the rest of the face hasn't committed yet. "That's rare. Most people in here are just being seen."

It's flattering. Of course it's flattering. He has taken the thing I was feeling ~ the loneliness of standing apart from a crowd, the slight self-consciousness of a woman who came alone ~ and he has reframed it as distinction. You're not separate from them because you don't fit. You're separate from them because you're better.

That's how it works, says the voice I'm still learning to trust. He found the wound and he put a gift in it.

You're being dramatic, says the other voice. The one that sounds like my ex-husband. He said something nice. That's allowed.

"It's a good piece," I say. My voice comes out steadier than I expected.

"It's derivative." He says it pleasantly, without cruelty. "But your face when you looked at it ~ that wasn't derivative. That was real."

My stomach tightens. I cannot tell if it is pleasure or warning. I am learning that these can feel identical, under the right conditions.

He extends his hand. "Lucian."

I take it. His grip is precise ~ not too firm, not too soft. The grip of a man who has practiced being exactly what the moment requires.

"Maya," I say.

He says my name back to me. He says it slowly, like he is tasting it, feeling its weight. Like he is deciding what to do with it.

"Maya." The faintest pause. "That's a name for someone who knows what she's looking at."

I don't know how to answer that. I tell him I'm a graphic designer, which is not what he asked. He listens with an attention that feels almost physical ~ the slight forward lean, the eye contact that doesn't break, the way he asks follow-up questions that prove he was actually listening to the answer before.

He tells me he sits on the board of the Winston Foundation. He says it casually. He is watching to see if I know what that means.

I know what it means. The Winston Foundation funds half the serious art and design work in this city. He could make a career. He knows I know this.

"You should come to the foundation's mixer next week," he says. "We're always looking for designers who actually see."

He says see the way you say a word when it means more than itself.

He is already holding out his phone. "What's your number?"

And this is the part I will think about later, in bed, staring at the ceiling: I give it to him. Not because I decide to. Because the sequence of things ~ his attention, the flattery, the professional opportunity, the phone already in his hand ~ creates a current, and I move with the current, and my fingers are typing my number before I have asked myself whether I want to.

He doesn't look at the screen. He is looking at my face.

"I'll see you next week, Maya."

He says it like a conclusion. Like an appointment already made.

Then he is gone, moving back through the crowd, and I am standing in front of a bruise-colored painting with my heart going too fast and my wine glass still in my hand and the sensation of his gaze still warm on the back of my neck like something that has not yet decided to let go.

I stand there for another ten minutes. I walk through the typography exhibit in the back without seeing any of it. I call a car. I go home. I lock my door.

I stand in my apartment ~ my small, careful apartment with its stacks of design books and its single window looking onto a brick wall ~ and I try to name what I am feeling.

The honest answer is: I felt seen.

The honest answer is also: something is wrong.

Both of these are true at the same time, and this is the thing nobody tells you ~ that the danger is not that it feels bad. The danger is that it feels like exactly what you have been starving for. The danger is that the wolf has learned to come in the shape of what you are missing.

I take out my journal. I write:

A man named Lucian at the gallery tonight. He noticed me. He made me feel like being noticed was a gift rather than a transaction. I can't tell if I'm grateful or afraid. Maybe those aren't different things.

I close the journal. I lie awake.

I do not dream of wolves. Not yet.

I dream of a bruise-colored painting and a woman standing in front of it, and the feeling of eyes that have found their target and are simply waiting, now, for the target to come closer.

CHAPTER 15:

The first day, I told myself it was nothing. Important men don't text the next day. They have things to do. I was not sitting by my phone.

I checked it eleven times before noon.

The second day, I told myself I had misread the whole encounter. The professional opportunity was genuine ~ he extended it to dozens of people, probably. He was on the board of a major foundation. He met a hundred graphic designers a year. My number was already forgotten.

I said his name in the shower. Lucian. I said it the way you say a word when you are trying to understand what kind of word it is.

The third day, I decided I was relieved. It meant nothing would have to happen. It meant I would not have to decide whether to trust the feeling in my chest or the cold feeling in my spine. Both feelings were exhausting. Silence resolved them both.

I was drafting copy for a bakery that had decided to call itself Yeast of Burden when my phone buzzed.

Unknown: The typography exhibit was forgettable. But the woman in front of the grief painting was not. Dinner Thursday? I know a place.

I read it three times.

I looked for something wrong with it. Something I could point to and say: here, this, this is the thing. But it was a perfectly ordinary text. A compliment, a direct question, an offer. Nothing in it should have made my palms cold.

And yet.

You're looking for reasons to be afraid, said the voice that sounds like my ex-husband. A handsome, successful man asked you to dinner. That is not a threat. That is what you said you wanted. That is what normal looks like.

I typed back: Thursday works. Where should I meet you?

The response came in seconds. Not a restaurant name. An address. A street and a number in a part of the city I didn't know well.

Lucian: You'll like it. I'll take care of everything.

I stared at those seven words for a long time.

I'll take care of everything.

It was meant to be reassuring. I understood that. He was telling me not to worry about logistics, not to research the menu, not to do the pre-date anxiety spiral of choosing wrong and seeming unsophisticated.

But what I heard, underneath the reassurance, was something else:

I am already making decisions for you. And I expect you to be comfortable with that.

I saved the address to my maps. I called Mel.

CHAPTER 16:

The address was in the old warehouse district, on a street where the buildings had been converted into things that didn't advertise themselves. A black door. A single brass handle. A light above it that cast more shadow than it dispelled.

No name. No sign. No window.

You're being dramatic, I told myself, standing on the sidewalk in the November cold. Private restaurants exist. Rich people do this. It doesn't mean anything.

I pulled open the door.

Inside ~ velvet and low light and the specific hush of a room designed to make you feel that the outside world has been suspended. A hostess in black led me through a sequence of small rooms, each more private than the last, until we reached a booth at the back. Leather. A candle. The architectural intimacy of a space that had been designed to make two people feel they were the only people.

Lucian was already there.

He stood when I arrived. The gesture was so precisely calibrated ~ gentlemanly, slightly old-fashioned, the kind of thing that makes a woman feel she is being treated with a care the modern world has forgotten ~ that I noticed the calculation in it even as I responded to it. He had worn a dark sweater instead of a suit. Deliberately casual. Deliberately more real.

"Maya." He said my name like he had been holding it. "You came."

"You said you knew a place."

"I do." He gestured to the booth. "No one bothers you here."

I slid in. The leather was cool. The table between us was smaller than I would have chosen.

"You look nervous," he said.

I was about to say I'm not, which would have been a lie, and something made me not want to start with a lie. "I don't usually go to restaurants without windows."

He tilted his head. The faintest smile. "You prefer to see what's coming."

Not a question. The way he said it suggested he found this both understandable and interesting ~ the way you find a lock interesting when you already have the key.

"I prefer daylight," I said. "That's all."

He nodded slowly, like I had confirmed something. "Daylight is safe," he said. "But safe is rarely where anything interesting happens."

He picked up the wine list and set it down without looking at it. "Do you trust me to order?"

The correct answer was: I just met you, so no. The answer I gave was: "Yes."

He signaled the waiter without looking away from my face.

He ordered in French. He knew the sommelier's name. He made small, precise adjustments to the proposed menu ~ not in the manner of someone being difficult, but in the manner of someone who has been here before, who has preferences, who expects them to be accommodated. The waiter accommodated them with the efficiency of someone who has learned that this particular guest's preferences are worth accommodating.

I watched this and I thought: he has a whole world. An entire infrastructure of people who know his name and his preferences and his history. And I know nothing about him except the shape of his gaze from twenty feet away and the sound of my name in his mouth.

"You went quiet," Lucian said, when the waiter had gone.

"I was thinking."

"About what?"

"About how much you know about this place and how little I know about you."

Something moved behind his eyes. It was fast ~ a flash of something that might have been assessment, might have been appreciation ~ and then it was gone.

"That's easy to fix," he said. "Ask me anything."

So I asked. And here is what I learned about Lucian Voss over the course of three hours and two bottles of wine in a restaurant with no windows:

He was an architect. He had studied in Europe. He had designed buildings in four countries, none of which he named specifically. He sat on the boards of three foundations. He had been married once, briefly, to a woman he described as someone who wanted a performance rather than a person.

He did not tell me the name of a single friend. He did not mention a family, except to say his parents were gone. He did not describe a home, a neighborhood, a daily life. He spoke fluently about ideas, about architecture, about art, about what it meant to truly see ~ but the actual texture of his existence, the small specific details that make a person real, were entirely absent.

I noticed this. I almost said something about it.

Instead, I talked about myself. And I talked and talked, drawn out by his questions, by the quality of his attention, by the way he made everything I said seem not just interesting but significant. I told him about the divorce. I told him about the graphic design work I actually cared about, as opposed to the work that paid for things. I told him about my mother. I told him ~ and this is the one I will come back to, the one that matters ~ I told him about the gaslighting. About the way my ex-husband had spent years making me doubt my own memory. About the journal I kept to hold onto what was real.

Lucian listened. He didn't interrupt. He didn't offer solutions. When I finished, he was quiet for a moment.

"That sounds like living in a house where someone has been moving the furniture an inch at a time," he said. "Until you stop trusting your own sense of where things are."

I stared at him. That was ~ exactly. That was exactly what it had felt like.

"I would never do that," he said. His voice was soft. Certain. "If I care about someone, I don't need them to doubt themselves. I need them to be exactly who they are. Doubt makes people smaller. I'm not interested in small."

He reached across the table. His hand covered mine. Warm. Dry. Deliberate.

"You're not broken, Maya. You were with someone who needed you to believe you were. That's different."

My throat tightened. No one had said it quite like that. My therapist used clinical language. Mel called Mark a jerk. But Lucian had taken the thing I had been trying to explain for two years and he had named it simply, without drama, like it was obvious.

And somewhere underneath the gratitude ~ underneath the almost unbearable relief of being understood ~ a small, cold voice said: he asked about your ex-husband on the first date. He found the wound. He knew exactly what to put in it.

I pushed the voice down. I smiled. I said thank you.

He walked me out at the end of the night. He didn't try to come in. He stood on the sidewalk, hands in his pockets, and looked at me in the cold air.

"I had a good time," he said.

"So did I."

He leaned in. I thought he was going to kiss me. Instead he pressed his lips to my forehead ~ soft, brief, the gesture of a man who knows that restraint is more powerful than contact.

"Goodnight, Maya."

He walked away. I stood in the cold and watched him go and tried to sort out what I was feeling from what I was supposed to be feeling, and couldn't find the seam between them.

In the car home, I texted Mel: He's too perfect.

She texted back within seconds: Too perfect how?

I stared at my phone. I didn't know how to answer. Not yet.

I typed: I'll tell you tomorrow. And I looked out the window at the city moving past and I thought about a man who knew exactly what to say and told me nothing about himself and I let the feeling sit in my chest without trying to name it.

I was still learning to let the feeling be a feeling before I turned it into a conclusion.

CHAPTER 17:

Mel came over the next evening with Thai food and a bottle of wine and the expectant face of a woman who has been waiting twenty-four hours for details.

"Too perfect," she said, settling onto my couch. "Explain."

I tried. I told her about the restaurant ~ no windows, no sign, no name. She said private dining was a thing. I told her he ordered for me. She pointed out I had said yes. I told her he was charming in a way that felt practiced. She tilted her head and said: "Isn't all charm practiced? That's what charm is."

She was not wrong. And yet.

"He didn't tell me anything real about himself," I said finally. "Three hours of conversation and I don't know where he lives or who his friends are or what he does on a Sunday morning. I know he has opinions about architecture and that his marriage ended badly. That's it."

Mel considered this. "Some people are private."

"He wasn't private. He was ~ present. He asked questions. He listened. He just never answered anything that would let me actually find him."

She was quiet for a moment. Then she pulled out her phone and found his Instagram ~ or what appeared to be his Instagram: a curated grid of buildings, black-tie events, a candid shot in a foreign city where he was looking over his shoulder at the camera, smiling.

"He looks," she said slowly, and then stopped.

"What?"

She shook her head. "Nothing. I was going to say something harsh."

"Say it."

She looked at the screen for another moment. "He looks like he's wearing a costume. Like every photo has been thought about. Nothing spontaneous." She set her phone down. "But that's not a crime, Maya. Some people are just very self-aware."

I stared at her. She had used my exact words ~ wearing a costume ~ without knowing I had been thinking them. The private alignment of two people who had known each other long enough to reach the same conclusion independently.

Or something else. I didn't know.

"You're doing it again," Mel said.

"Doing what?"

"Looking for the evidence. The thing that proves he's dangerous." Her voice was gentle. Patient. The voice she used when she thought I was spiraling. "Maya. You've been on one date. He was charming and attentive and professional and he kissed you on the forehead like you were worth being careful with. That's not a red flag. That's a man who's interested."

"I know. I know you're right."

"But?"

I looked at my wine. "Something felt wrong. I can't say what. Just ~ wrong."

Mel leaned forward. She looked at me with the focused attention she brought to things that mattered to her, and I felt, as I always felt under that attention, simultaneously seen and steadied.

"Your ex spent eight years teaching you that wrong feelings were proof you were broken," she said. "So now you don't know if a wrong feeling is a genuine alarm or just ~ residue. Right?"

"Yes," I said. "Exactly that."

"Then you go on a second date. You gather information. You don't decide anything yet." She topped up my glass. "You give the thing a chance to be what it is before you decide what it is."

I nodded. She was reasonable. She was kind. She had been saying reasonable, kind things to me for fifteen years and had almost never been wrong.

I went home and I took out my journal and I wrote:

Mel says go on a second date. She says I don't know the difference anymore between a real alarm and residue. She might be right. She's usually right.

I paused. Then I wrote:

She used the same words I was thinking. Wearing a costume. I hadn't said that to her. She just ~ said it. That happens with people you've known a long time. Or it means something else. I don't know which.

I closed the journal. I went to sleep. I dreamed of a grid of photographs, each one perfectly composed, a man looking over his shoulder at the camera with a smile that said: I know you're there. I've always known.

CHAPTER 18:

The flower arrived at my office four days after the first date.

I was at my desk, drafting the final logo options for Yeast of Burden (the client had decided they wanted something that "felt artisanal but also a little dangerous," which was not a design brief so much as a personality crisis), when my phone buzzed.

Lucian: I've been thinking about what you said. About learning to trust yourself again. I think you're braver than you know.

I read it twice. It was the right thing to say ~ the perfectly right thing, referencing something specific from our conversation, framing it as admiration rather than pity. I felt the warmth of it and I felt, underneath the warmth, the now-familiar discomfort of not being able to separate the thing that felt good from the thing that felt off.

I typed back: That's kind of you to say.

He responded: It's not kindness. It's observation.

Then, twenty minutes later, the receptionist appeared in my doorway. "There's something at the front desk for you."

A single stem. White. In a glass vase that someone had placed, the receptionist said, at the front desk sometime that morning. No card. No delivery note. No florist's tag.

"Who brought it?" I asked.

She frowned. "It was just there when I came in. I thought you left it yourself."

I carried the vase to my desk. I sat in front of it for a long time.

I had not told Lucian where I worked. I had mentioned the bakery client. I had mentioned a rebranding project. I had said graphic design without naming a firm or a street or a floor number.

I picked up my phone. I started to type: Did you send me a flower?

I stopped.

Don't, said the voice. If you ask, he'll have an answer. He will have found out through a mutual contact, or he'll say a friend knew someone at your firm, or he'll say he did some research because he was interested and wasn't that a natural thing to do. He will have an answer that sounds reasonable. You will feel foolish for asking. And the flower will still be on your desk and you still won't know how it got there.

I put my phone down. I worked around the flower for the rest of the day. I didn't throw it away.

That night, I wrote in my journal:

He sent a flower to my office. He doesn't know where my office is. Or he didn't, until he found out. I don't know when he found out or how. I don't know if I should ask.

I paused for a long time. Then:

I didn't ask. I'm not sure if that's because I've gotten better at managing anxiety or because some part of me already knows I won't like the answer.

CHAPTER 19:

The second dates restaurant had windows. Floor to ceiling, looking out onto a garden strung with lights. It was beautiful. It was exactly the opposite of the first place.

He had chosen it because of what I said. I prefer daylight. He had heard that, filed it, and made the adjustment. He was paying attention to me in a way that felt like care and also, if I held it at a certain angle, like research.

He was already there when I arrived. He stood when he saw me ~ the same gesture as before, the old-fashioned courtesy ~ and this time he looked, I thought, genuinely pleased. Not the composed pleasure of the first date, but something warmer. Less controlled.

"I wasn't sure you'd come," he said.

"Why not?"

"You seemed uncertain. When we texted." He pulled out my chair. "I thought maybe I'd moved too fast."

"You sent a flower to my office," I said. "I never told you where I worked."

I had not planned to say it. But there it was, between us, and I watched his face with the careful attention of someone who has learned to look for the thing underneath the expression.

He sat. He met my eyes. He looked ~ and this is what I could not resolve ~ genuinely surprised.

"I called the gallery," he said. "The one where we met. I asked if they knew any graphic designers in the area who'd attended that particular opening. The coordinator remembered you and said you worked at Fielding." He paused. "I should have said something. I can see how that would feel strange."

The answer was smooth. It was specific. It had the texture of something true.

"It did feel strange," I said.

"I'm sorry." He looked at me steadily, no deflection. "I was impatient. I wanted to reach you before you talked yourself out of the second date. That was ~ presumptuous. I understand if it bothered you."

He apologized. Without qualification, without turning it back on me, without adding a but. In eight years of marriage I had received approximately four apologies, all of them eventually followed by however.

I told myself, “an apology is not proof. A smooth answer is not proof of innocence”. But I let myself sit with it.

"How did you know I was talking myself out of it?" I asked.

His mouth curved. "Because you're careful. And careful people always find reasons not to move toward something new." He picked up the menu. "It's a strength, mostly. Sometimes it's a cage."

I looked at him across the table. I thought: he is either a man who understands me unusually well, or a man who is very skilled at creating the impression of understanding. And I do not yet know which one I am sitting across from.

I decided to find out.

The second date lasted three hours. The windows made everything feel more honest ~ no velvet seclusion, no manufactured privacy. Just a table and two people and the ordinary world moving past the glass.

He told me more about himself this time. Still no friends, no specific addresses, no texture of daily life ~ but more about his work, about the buildings he had designed, about what architecture meant to him as a discipline. He spoke about it with the passion of someone who had genuinely thought about something for a long time.

"A building is a promise," he said. "It says: someone thought about what a human being needs, and tried to give it to them. Space. Light. The feeling of being held without being constrained."

"That's a generous way to think about it."

"Most things are generous if you look at them that way."

I looked at him. "What's an ungenerous way to think about architecture?"

He paused. Something moved behind his eyes ~ interest, or the simulation of it. "That a building is just a demonstration of power. Someone deciding what a space will be and forcing everyone inside to live inside that decision."

"Which is it?"

"Both," he said. "Depending on the architect."

He smiled. I smiled. We ate the excellent food and drank the excellent wine and talked about everything and nothing, and I kept waiting for the thing that would tip the balance ~ that would let me decide, one way or the other, what I was dealing with.

At the end of the night he walked me to my car. He didn't try to kiss me. He stood in the cold and looked at me with an expression I couldn't read.

"I'd like to see you again," he said.

"I'd like that too," I said, and as I said it I checked whether it was true. It was. Which was either evidence that I was healing and learning to receive good things, or evidence that the thing I was most afraid of was already working.

I couldn't tell.

I drove home. I didn't write in my journal that night.

Some things I was not ready to put into words.

CHAPTER 20:

The third date was Lucian's choice. Italian, a place where the tables were far enough apart to suggest that privacy was being sold alongside the food. The lighting was the particular warm dimness of restaurants that know their clientele prefers a little softening.

The waiter was young. Eager. The kind of eager that comes from caring about the job and not yet knowing which customers will punish you for it.

He recommended a Barolo with some confidence ~ their most popular, he said, excellent value, very popular with the regulars. He said it with the genuine enthusiasm of someone who had been told to develop knowledge and had done so.

Lucian's expression didn't change. That was the thing. Nothing moved in his face. But something shifted in the air around him, the almost imperceptible change in atmospheric pressure that comes before weather.

"Barolo," he repeated.

"Yes, sir. It's really~"

"You looked at me," Lucian said pleasantly, "and you thought: popular. You thought: accessible. You thought: this is a man who wants what other men want." He tilted his head. "Is that what I look like to you?"

The waiter's smile faltered. He recalibrated. "I didn't mean~"

"I know." Lucian waved a hand ~ a gesture of absolution that somehow made it worse. "Bring the Barolo. We'll pretend this was the recommendation and not the default."

He laughed. The waiter laughed, too high and too fast, the laugh of someone who has been caught in something they don't fully understand and is hoping laughter will be the exit.

Lucian looked at me. He was expecting me to laugh too.

I smiled. It felt tight on my face.

When the waiter had gone, Lucian leaned forward. "He'll learn," he said. "You can't read people if you're not willing to actually look at them."

"He was trying to be helpful," I said.

"He was trying to be efficient. There's a difference." Lucian poured water into my glass. Unbothered. "Don't feel sorry for him. He'll be better at his job for it."

I looked at my menu. I thought about the waiter's face ~ the way it had gone through four expressions in three seconds, the way the eager brightness had collapsed and then reassembled into something more careful. I thought about what it felt like to be in a conversation and suddenly understand that the ground has shifted and you are being assessed rather than spoken to.

I knew that feeling. I knew it from the inside.

And I thought: that's what you look like, said a voice in my head, quiet and steady, the voice I had been practicing trusting. That's exactly what you look like when he corrects your reality. When he says you're imagining things. When he makes you feel that the most reasonable interpretation of events is the one he provides.

You smile. Just like the waiter. You laugh too fast. You let him redefine what just happened.

I looked at Lucian across the table. He was examining the wine list with a calm, pleasant expression, entirely at ease.

I thought: this is who he is when he thinks he's safe.

I thought: remember this.

CHAPTER 21:

After the third date, he drove me home. He had insisted ~ my car was in the shop, a convenient timing ~ and I had said yes before considering whether I wanted him to know where I lived.

He already knows, said a voice. He found your office with a phone call. Your address is not harder.

I told the voice to wait.

He parked outside my building. He got out, walked around, opened my door ~ the performance of courtesy was flawless, consistent, never varying. I had started to find its consistency more unsettling than its absence would have been.

We stood on the sidewalk. The night was cold. He looked at me with an expression I still couldn't fully read ~ something between warmth and appraisal, the two things so layered in him that I had stopped trying to separate them.

"I have something for you," he said.

He reached into his coat pocket and produced a small box. Matte black. When he opened it: a key. Old. Brass, tarnished to the color of old pennies, hanging on a leather cord. A skeleton key ~ the kind that opens things that have been closed for a long time.

"What is this?" I asked.

"A key to a building I'm renovating. In the warehouse district." He lifted it from the box and, without asking, slipped it over my head. It settled against my collarbone, cool and heavier than I expected. "It's empty right now. Just walls and potential. I go there when I need to think."

I touched it. The metal was smooth, worn, the warmth of use absorbed into it over years. "You're giving me a key to a building I've never seen."

"I'm giving you a key to a place I don't show people." He looked at me with an intensity that I had learned to brace for ~ the look that said: this moment is significant. "I want you to be able to go there. Whether I'm there or not. I want you to know that with me, doors open."

I should have said: it's too much, too soon. I should have said: I don't want a symbol, I want information. I should have taken it off and handed it back.

He kissed me then. Not the forehead this time ~ my mouth, soft and brief and asking nothing immediately, the kiss of a man who is making a deposit rather than a withdrawal.

When he pulled back his hands were on my face. His thumbs at my jaw. His eyes very close, very pale in the streetlight.

"Goodnight, Maya."

He walked back to his car. I stood on the sidewalk with the key against my chest and I told myself: this is a nice thing. A man gave you a key. That is a gesture of trust.

But I stood there for a long time after his car had turned the corner.

The key was cool against my skin.

I thought about locks. About buildings. About a man who chooses what opens and what stays closed.

About who, exactly, was being let in.

CHAPTER 22:

That night I wrote for a long time.

Three dates. Here is what I know about Lucian Voss:

He is an architect. He sits on the boards of three foundations. He was married once and it ended badly ~ his word, badly, with no further detail. He speaks French. He doesn't like to be given what other people are given. He apologized once, cleanly, without qualification. He sends flowers to addresses he finds through channels he doesn't fully disclose. He gives keys to buildings he owns as symbols of trust. He makes waiters feel small and calls it education.

Here is what I don't know:

Where he lives. Who his friends are. What he does alone. What he is afraid of. What he has lost. What he regrets. Whether the warmth is a layer or whether it goes all the way through.

Here is what my body knows:

Something is wrong. My body has been saying this since the gallery and I keep finding reasons to disagree with it. I keep deciding it's residue ~ my ex's voice, my ex's lessons. I keep deciding that the warmth is real and the cold underneath it is a malfunction.

But here is what I also know: my body has been trying to tell me things for a long time. And every time I have listened to the voice that says you're imagining it, I have been wrong.

I closed the journal. I held the key in my palm for a moment. I thought about putting it in a drawer.

I put it back around my neck.

I still can't explain why. Maybe I thought keeping it close meant keeping it where I could see it. Maybe I thought that giving it back would signal something I wasn't ready to signal.

Maybe I already knew, in the way the body knows before the mind allows it, that the key was not a gift.

It was a claim.

CHAPTER 23:

The fourth date, and the fifth, and the sixth.

Lucian was patient in the way that rivers are patient ~ not still, but persistent, wearing at the edges of things so gradually that you don't notice the shape changing until you look back at what it used to be.

He texted every morning. Not effusively ~ just enough. A line about something he'd read. A question about my work. Once, a photograph of a building detail ~ an old hinge, ornate and slightly rusted ~ with no caption. I looked at it for five minutes before I understood: he was thinking of me. He was telling me he was thinking of me in a language that didn't require him to say so.

It was intimate. It was also entirely controlled.

The cracks appeared slowly. Not in him ~ his surface remained smooth. The cracks appeared in me: small fissures between what I felt and what I thought I should feel, between the warmth he gave me and the cold I felt underneath it.

The fourth date: he talked about his ex-wife. "She wanted a version of me," he said. "A curated version. When I stopped performing it, she left." He said it without apparent bitterness, which somehow made it worse. As if he had processed it so thoroughly that it no longer touched him. As if nothing quite touched him. "She was afraid of the real thing."

"What's the real thing?" I asked.

He looked at me across the table with those pale, assessing eyes. "That's what you're trying to find out," he said. "Isn't it."

Not a question.

The fifth date: he mentioned my divorce unprompted, referencing something I had said on the first date ~ a specific detail about the way Mark had rewritten events. He had been holding it. He had been holding everything I had said, I realized. The conversation had been a filing cabinet, not an exchange.

"You said he used to tell you that you were the one with the problem," Lucian said. "That if you were different, things would be better."

I had said this. Weeks ago. I didn't remember saying it.

"Yes," I said carefully.

"I think about that." He looked at his wine. "I think about someone taking a person who sees clearly ~ and I mean really sees, the way you do, the way you looked at that painting the first night ~ and spending years convincing her that the seeing is a malfunction. How much damage that does." He looked up. "How long it takes to trust your own eyes again."

He was right. He was saying something true. And the truth of it was the mechanism: he was using what I had told him to build a portrait of me as someone damaged, who needed restoration, who was lucky to be seen now by someone who understood.

I felt the gratitude and I felt, underneath it, the slow slide of something I couldn't name.

The sixth date: he arrived at the restaurant twenty minutes late. No text. No explanation until he sat down, and even then, just: "Something came up. Are you all right?"

I said I was fine. I was not fine. Twenty minutes is twenty minutes, and I had spent them doing what I did not want to admit I had been doing ~ second-guessing myself. Wondering if I had the wrong restaurant. Wondering if I had the wrong time. Reaching for my phone to check the messages and check them again and double-check, in the way you do when you have spent enough time with someone who moves the furniture that you no longer trust your own sense of where things are.

"Something came up" remained the full explanation.

I didn't ask what. I should have asked what. I didn't ask because somewhere in the weeks of his patient attention I had started to believe ~ without examining the belief ~ that asking questions he hadn't offered to answer was the kind of behavior that would cost me something.

That night, for the first time, I didn't tell Mel about the date.

When she texted to ask, I said it was fine. Nice. Nothing particular to report.

I sat with that for a while afterward: the fact that I had started editing. The fact that I was protecting the story because examining it felt dangerous ~ not dangerous in the way of a man who might hurt me, but dangerous in the way of a mirror you are not ready to look in.

I opened my journal. I wrote one line:

I'm shrinking. I can feel it. And I don't know if that's healing or the opposite.

CHAPTER 24:

On the seventh date, Lucian asked about my divorce. Not casually. He waited until we were walking along the river path, the evening light going gold, my guard softened by the beauty of it and the accumulated warmth of weeks of careful attention.

"Why did it really end?" he asked. "Not the version you tell people. The real one."

I thought about not answering. Then I thought: this is what trust looks like. This is what it costs.

I told him. More than I had told him before. The years of small erasures. The way Mark would rewrite events after the fact, so consistently and confidently that I had started to believe his versions over my own. The way I kept a journal ~ writing things down immediately, while they were fresh, because his version would come later and it would be so reasonable and so certain that without the original record I would lose my grip on what had actually happened.

Lucian listened. When I finished, he said: "That's not a difficult marriage. That's abuse."

I stopped walking. "I don't know if I'd call it~"

"He made you doubt your own mind." Lucian stopped too, turning to face me. His voice was quiet. Measured. "That's what abusers do. They take the one thing you're supposed to be able to trust ~ your own perception of reality ~ and they dismantle it, piece by piece, so slowly you don't notice until you're relying on them to tell you what's true. So you can't leave. Because you've forgotten you're the one who knows things."

I stared at him. "How do you know that?"

"I've seen it. Someone I loved, a long time ago." Something moved in his jaw ~ a tightening, a restraint. He looked away, toward the river. "I watched it happen and I couldn't stop it. I swore I would never be someone who did that to a person."

The words were exactly right. They were so exactly right that I noticed, in a distant and quickly suppressed way, that I had forgotten to notice they were also his answer to my question deflected into a story about himself.

I had asked how he knew. He had told me what he had promised.

These were not the same thing.

"He was wrong about you," Lucian said. He stepped closer. His hand found mine. "You're not broken. You were with someone who needed you to be, and that's different. And anyone who tells you otherwise doesn't deserve to be in the same room as you."

My throat tightened. I almost cried. The truth of it moved through me ~ the thing I had needed to hear, the permission I had been waiting years for someone to give me.

I am not broken.

And then, underneath that, a different voice: he heard what you needed. He is giving it to you. Watch.

Three days later I saw him outside the warehouse.

It was late. Almost midnight. I was driving back through the warehouse district ~ a printing emergency, a client who had changed her mind for the fourth time ~ and I was at a red light when I saw him.

Lucian, on the sidewalk outside a gray brick building. Not alone.

A woman. Young. Blonde hair, a coat pulled tight. She was talking with the urgency of someone who needs to be heard ~ her hands moving, her body leaning in ~ and he was standing very still, watching her speak the way you watch something you are deciding about.

His face.

I had been looking at his face for weeks. I knew the warmth of it, the precision of it, the performance of attention. What I was looking at now was none of those things.

His face was empty. The warmth was gone as if it had never existed. What was left was something I had no immediate word for ~ not cruel, not angry, something more fundamental. The face of a person who has stopped performing entirely because they believe no one is watching.

The woman touched his arm. He didn't react. She said something that made her voice rise ~ I could hear the elevation even through the glass ~ and he moved. Just a shift of weight, a single step forward. The woman stepped back. Her hands came up, palms out.

Fear. Her body was expressing fear.

The light turned green. I did not move.

Lucian turned. His eyes swept the street in the automatic way of a man assessing his environment, and then they found my car. Found me, sitting at the green light, watching him.

For one second ~ one long, cold, freezing second ~ we looked at each other. And I saw his face do the thing I will not forget for as long as I live. I saw the mask return. Not gradually, not with any transition. Like a light switched on: the warmth was back, the pleasantness was back, the man who listened and remembered and told you that you were rare was back.

He raised his hand. He waved. Easy. Warm. As if I had caught him doing something entirely ordinary.

I drove. My hands were shaking. I drove for twenty minutes and then I pulled over and I sat with the engine running and I looked at my own hands on the steering wheel.

I knew what I had seen. I had seen it before, from the inside ~ the face that emerges when someone believes they are not being observed. I knew the quality of it. I knew what it meant.

I picked up my phone. I texted him.

Maya: I saw you tonight. Downtown. Outside a building. Who was that woman?

The response came in forty seconds.

Lucian: What woman?

I read it twice. I read it the way you read something that doesn't make sense.

Maya: The woman you were with. Outside the warehouse building. She looked frightened.

Lucian: Maya, I've been home all evening. I think you must have seen someone else.

I put my phone face-down on the passenger seat. I picked it up again.

Maya: You saw me. You waved.

Three dots appeared. Disappeared. Appeared again. The wait was longer this time. Calculated.

Lucian: I want to be honest with you, because I think you deserve honesty. And because I think what your ex-husband did to you deserves to be named for what it is.

Lucian: You've been under significant stress. The move. The divorce. Coming back to a city that has a lot of difficult associations. And I know ~ I know how hard you've worked to trust yourself again. How much courage that takes.

Lucian: I just wonder ~ and I say this with care, not criticism ~ whether sometimes the work of rebuilding trust can tip into... looking for confirmation of what we're already afraid of. Whether sometimes we see things that fit our fears because our fears are very loud.

Lucian: I was home. I have timestamps on my work emails if you need to see them. But I don't think what you need right now is my alibi. I think what you need is to be gentle with yourself.

I sat in the dark of my car and I read the messages three times.

And this is the thing: he wasn't wrong about any individual piece. I was under stress. I had been told so many times by my ex-husband that my perception was broken that I genuinely did not always trust it. The divorce had been hard. The city had associations.

He had taken every true thing and assembled them into a shape that put the evidence inside my head.

I saw what I saw, said the voice.

You've been wrong before, said the other voice. You've been so wrong before.

The two voices in my head. One of them mine. One of them his, by now so thoroughly installed that I couldn't always tell the difference.

I drove home. I sat at my kitchen table. I took out my journal and I wrote down everything ~ the time, the street, the building, the woman's hands coming up, the mask sliding back. I wrote it in full, in the present tense, the way I had learned to write things when I needed them to stay real.

Then I wrote:

He used my divorce to make me doubt what I saw with my own eyes. He knew exactly where to press. He knew because I told him. I gave him the map.

And then, because I am a woman who has learned the hard way to document:

I know what I saw. I saw his real face. I saw the woman afraid of him. I saw the mask come back on. I know what I saw.

I closed the journal. I put it under my mattress, not on my nightstand. Something had shifted, though I couldn't yet name the full shape of it.

I had stopped trusting the room.

CHAPTER 25:

I didn't text him the next morning. When his good morning message arrived ~ Hope you slept well. Thinking of you ~ I looked at it for a long time and then put my phone face-down.

At lunch I drafted the message. I want to take some space. I don't think this is working for me. I rewrote it six times, making it more neutral each time, removing anything he could argue with. I want to focus on work right now. I think we should take a step back.

Cowardly. I knew it was cowardly. But I also knew that naming what I had seen would hand him another map ~ another inventory of my fears, another set of coordinates for where to press next.

Before I could send it, my phone rang. Lucian.

I answered. I don't know why I answered.

"Maya." His voice was warm, concerned. The voice of a man who was worried about someone he cared for. "I've been thinking about last night. About what I said."

I said nothing.

"I don't want you to feel like I was dismissing you. I wasn't. What you felt ~ the disorientation, the doubt ~ that's real. I'm not telling you your feelings are wrong." A pause. The pause of a man who has thought about what comes next. "I'm just saying that I wasn't there. I was home. And I'm concerned that something is making it hard for you to hold onto that."

Something is making it hard. Not someone. Something. Unnamed, sourceless, a problem that exists inside me.

"I saw you," I said.

"I know you believe that." His voice was gentle. The gentleness of a man managing something fragile. "And I believe that you believe it. That's not the same as it being true."

The silence after that was the loudest kind.

"I'm going to take some space," I said.

"Of course. Take all the space you need." Another pause. Then, quietly: "I'll be here. That's not a threat or a demand. I just want you to know. When you're ready."

He hung up gently. I sat at my desk and looked at the Yeast of Burden logo and thought about what it meant that an apology and a manipulation could sound so similar when delivered by the right voice.

I thought about what it meant that I was still not sure which one it had been.

Mel called that afternoon. I told her I had pulled back. She asked why. I told her about the warehouse, the woman, the messages.

"Are you sure it was him?" she said.

My heart stopped.

"It was him, Mel."

"I believe you. I do. I just ~ it was dark, you were tired, you said yourself you've been under a lot of stress~"

"You sound like him."

A silence. Long enough to matter.

"Maya. I'm not trying to~"

"I know." I pressed my hand to my eyes. "I know you're not. I'm sorry. I'm just ~ I need to think."

"Of course. Take your time. Call me if you need anything."

She was kind. She was worried. She was saying all the right things.

And yet she had also, in those few sentences, said almost exactly what he had said. You were tired. You were stressed. Are you sure.

Two people, both of whom I trusted, pointing in the same direction.

I sat with that for a long time.

Then I took out my journal ~ the one under the mattress ~ and I opened it to what I had written the night before.

I read my own words. Present tense. Specific. The time, the street, the building, the woman's hands, the mask.

I read it three times.

Then I wrote:

I am not going to disappear. I'm going to find out what I actually saw.

I looked at the key around my neck. The tarnished brass of it. The leather cord.

I thought about the building. The building Lucian was renovating. The building he had given me a key to as a symbol ~ he had said symbol ~ of trust.

I thought: I have a key. And I know the address.

I thought: maybe it's time to see what the symbol opens.

CHAPTER 26: MEL

Maya was drowning when I found her.

That is not dramatic. That is the literal truth. She was sitting on a bench outside the library, twenty years old, crying over a boy whose name I have already forgotten ~ some boy, some ordinary careless boy who had done the ordinary careless thing of choosing someone else. She looked up at me when I sat down beside her and her face did something I had never seen on another person's face before and have never seen since.

It opened. Just opened, like a window in a closed room. Like I was air.

Like I was exactly what she needed, arriving at exactly the right moment.

I have thought about that moment many times over the years. The specific quality of it. The way she looked at me as if I were something she had been waiting for without knowing she was waiting. I have thought about what it means that I recognized that look ~ that I knew, immediately and instinctively, what it was and what it required of me.

I sat down. I didn't think about it. I just sat, because sitting beside a drowning person is the obvious thing to do if you are the kind of person who notices drowning.

I am that kind of person. I have always been that kind of person. My mother was that kind of person ~ she collected people the way some people collect objects, kept them on shelves, tended them with obsessive care. The difference between my mother and me is that I have never pretended I wasn't holding on.

What I didn't understand, not for years, was that holding on and holding someone are not the same thing.

But I understood other things. I understood them early, and well, and I have spent a long time deciding what to do with that understanding.

Maya needed me. That is the simplest truth I know. She needed someone who would stay ~ who would show up at three in the morning and not keep score, who would remember what she said and build her up and dismantle the people who diminished her. And I was so good at that. I have always been good at that.

The problem is what happens when they stop needing you.

When she met Mark, I was worried. Not because he was cruel ~ I didn't know he was cruel yet ~ but because she was looking at him the way she used to look at me. Like he was air. And I knew, with the certainty of someone who has been studying a person for years, that he was not. He was just another person who would eventually choose something else.

I was wrong about that. He didn't choose something else. He chose to stay and to make her smaller and smaller until the version of her that existed was one that needed me again. Needed everyone, really, but especially me.

I know how that sounds.

I am going to tell you what I have never told anyone: when she called me from the parking garage of her office building, crying, the day she finally understood what her marriage was, part of me ~ a small, terrible part of me ~ felt something that was not entirely grief.

I felt the relief of a person who has been afraid of losing something and has just discovered they have not lost it yet.

I hate that part of me. I have always hated it. But hatred is not the same as absence. You can hate a thing that is still true.

My mother sat across from me at her kitchen table when I was sixteen and she said: Mel. The things you love don't belong to you. The sooner you understand that, the less damage you will do ...

I had known about Lucian way before Maya met him, in the way that certain people know about each other without having been introduced, the way that a specific quality in a person makes them visible to others who carry the same quality. I had seen his name. I had heard him described. I had understood, in the abstract, what he was and what he did, in the way that you understand a tool before you pick it up.

I am going to say this plainly, because I have spent fifteen years not saying it plainly and the weight of it has become something I carry in my body now, in my shoulders and the particular tension behind my eyes that never quite releases.

I knew what he was. I knew who he was. I knew what he did with women who were in transition, who were rebuilding, who had been taught to doubt their own perception. I knew the pattern ~ the galleries, the keys, the specific hunger he found in each of them and fed with surgical precision. I knew because I recognized it. Because I had been doing a version of it myself, in a smaller and more loving way, for years. Because it takes one to know one, and I had known, from the first time I heard his name, that we were reading from the same page.

That is the thing I have never said out loud.

That is the thing I am saying now, here, in the quiet of my apartment with the wine and the photographs and the specific silence of a person who has finally run out of room to run from herself.

Lena.

I am going to think about Lena now, clearly, without the management I usually apply to thinking about her.

She was Maya's person before I fully had Maya. That is the first fact. The second fact is that Lena saw things ~ she had that quality, the quality of genuine perception uncontaminated by the need to be liked or the fear of being difficult. She looked at people and she saw them and she said what she saw. It was one of the things Maya loved most about her.

It was the thing that made her a problem.

I watched her that night. At the gallery. I did not leave at nine ~ I left later, much later, after I had seen what I needed to see and understood that the situation was being handled. I stood near the second doorway, the one that led to the office corridor, and I watched a man with his hand on a girl's arm and the girl trying to move away, and I understood that this was the end of a particular problem.

I left because there was nothing left for me to do.

I have told myself, for fifteen years, that this is not the same as doing something. That watching is not participating. That standing near a doorway while something happens is not the same as the thing happening.

I have told myself this so many times that there are days I believe it.

Tonight is not one of those days.

Lena is gone. Maya is here. I have been holding these two facts in separate rooms for fifteen years and tonight, for the first time, I am allowing them to be in the same room together. I am looking at them side by side.

I am not going to describe what I see. Some things, even in the privacy of your own mind, you do not say plainly. Some things you approach and then step back from, because the full sight of them is more than the structure of a person can hold.

When Daniel came to me, four years after Lena disappeared, I told him what I told him. Enough to seem cooperative. Enough to seem like a woman carrying guilt rather than a woman managing information. I gave him the shape of a truth without its substance ~ a man, a hand, an arm, a girl trying to move away. All of it accurate. None of it complete.

He believed me.

But Maya is here now. And Maya is looking. And Maya has always been the one variable I could not fully predict, because Maya loves me, and love makes people both more and less likely to see clearly ~ more, because love pays attention; less, because love wants to find something other than what the evidence suggests.

I have been depending on the less. I am beginning to worry about the more.

The text arrives while I am on my second glass of wine.

Unknown: She's getting close. Time to decide which side you're on.

I read it. I set the phone down on the cushion beside me. I pick up my wine.

I do not feel afraid. That is the thing I notice ~ the absence of fear where fear would be reasonable, where fear would be the appropriate response of a person receiving a threatening message. What I feel instead is the particular clarity of a decision that has been approaching for a long time and has finally arrived.

I have always known this moment would come. I planned for it, in the abstract, the way you plan for weather ~ you cannot prevent it, you can only decide in advance how you will respond when it arrives.

I finish my wine. I look at the photographs of Maya on my wall. The graduation photograph. The beach. The wedding I attended knowing it was wrong, knowing what Mark was, sitting in the front row in a blue dress and smiling because this was what was required and I have always been able to produce what is required.

I think about what she looked like on the day her divorce was final. Sitting on my couch with bare feet and red eyes. The face of a woman who has lost the structure of her life and does not yet know what will replace it.

The relief I felt that day. The terrible, genuine, unforgivable relief.

I sit with it now. The shame and the relief both, occupying the same space, the way they have always occupied the same space ~ because they are not opposites. They are the same feeling, seen from different angles. The feeling of a person who has arranged things and watched them go according to plan.

I pick up my phone. I look at the message for a long time.

Then I type:

She's not as close as you think. I can manage it.

I send it. I set the phone face down. I finish what is left of my wine.

I look at the photographs of Maya on my wall and I try to locate, somewhere in myself, the version of this that is love. It is there. I know it is there. The love has always been real ~

that is the part that cannot be faked, the part that has never been strategy. I have loved her since she was twenty years old and drowning and her face opened like a window.

I have loved her and I have held her and I have steered her and I have kept her and I have told myself, for fifteen years, that these were all the same thing.

I am only now, in the quiet of this apartment, beginning to understand that they are not.

But understanding is not the same as stopping.

I know the difference between those two things. I have always known it.

I go to the kitchen. I open the drawer beside the sink ~ the one that holds batteries and takeout menus and the small miscellaneous objects of a life lived carefully. At the back, beneath everything else, a key. Old brass, tarnished to the color of old pennies, on a length of leather cord.

Not the one he gave Maya. A different one. An older one.

Mine.

I hold it for a moment. Then I put it back. I close the drawer.

I go to bed. I don't sleep for a long time.

When I do, I don't dream of Lena. I never dream of Lena.

That is the thing I am most afraid of, in the part of myself I am still honest with.

That I stopped dreaming of her a very long time ago.

CHAPTER 27:

I went on a Tuesday afternoon, when the street was quiet.

I had looked up the address from the key box. A building in the warehouse district, listed under a holding company that listed Lucian Voss as its sole director. The city planning database had it flagged as a long-term renovation project, permits renewed annually, no completion date on record.

A building that was always being worked on and never finished. I had written that in my journal and then stared at it for a while.

The key worked. Of course it worked ~ he had given it to me as a symbol, he had said, "doors opening." The irony of that was not lost on me as I pushed through the iron door into the dark of the warehouse interior.

The ground floor was empty in the way of a space that has been carefully emptied ~ no debris, no construction materials, just the bones of an old industrial building cleaned down to its skeleton. High ceilings. Concrete floors. A staircase along the far wall.

I went up.

The second floor was different. There was a table. On the table: permits, contracts, architectural drawings. On the walls: nothing yet. But there were hooks. A row of them, installed with the precision of someone who had measured and planned. Empty hooks, evenly spaced, running the length of the far wall.

Waiting for something.

I moved to the table. The documents were ordinary ~ building permits, city communications, contractor invoices.

But underneath them, at the bottom of the stack: a notebook. Small. Cloth-covered. Someone had left it here. It had not been forgotten; it had been placed.

I opened it.

The handwriting was not Lucian's. It was a woman's writing ~ small, careful, the writing of someone who had learned to take up less space than they needed. The notebook was mostly blank. But in the back, on the last page, pressed hard enough to leave an impression on the page beneath:

He's like a wolf. I can feel him watching me even when I can't see him. I thought it was love. I thought being seen was the same thing as being safe.

And below that, in the same hand, smaller:

If you found this, it means you have the key. It means he gave it to you as a gift and told you it meant he trusted you. It doesn't mean that. It means he has decided you're next.

It means run.

I closed the notebook. I stood in the empty warehouse with the city sounds coming up from the street and the row of empty hooks on the wall, and I breathed.

The hooks. I understood them now. A row of labeled hooks, waiting. Each one a key. Each key a woman. Each woman a story that ended the same way.

I took out my phone. I photographed every page of the notebook. I photographed the wall with its hooks. I photographed the table and the permits.

I put the notebook back exactly where I had found it. I went down the stairs. I went out the iron door.

On the street, I stood in the afternoon light and I made myself breathe.

The key was still around my neck.

I didn't take it off. Not yet. Not until I understood everything it opened.

I took out my phone. I called Daniel Sinclair.

"I went to the warehouse," I said when he answered. "I found a notebook. Someone left it there. A woman."

A pause. Then: "What did it say?"

"It said run."

The silence on the line was the silence of a man who has been trying to get someone to see something for a very long time and has just watched them finally see it.

"Come to the gallery," he said. "There's more you need to know."

I walked back through the warehouse district, past buildings being converted into lofts and galleries and coffee shops, past the ordinary afternoon life of people who were not carrying a key that wasn't a gift and a notebook that said run, past all of it, toward whatever was next.

Behind me, from an upper floor of the warehouse, I felt ~ or believed I felt, because by now I was paying attention to what I felt ~ the familiar cold along the back of my neck.

Eyes.

I didn't turn around.

I had learned, finally, not to turn around until I was somewhere safe.

But I noted it. I wrote it down in my journal that night.

He was watching me leave.

He was letting me.

That was the part I couldn't yet understand: why a man who did not want to be caught was letting me see exactly what he was.

I would understand it later. But later was not now.

Now I walked toward Daniel's gallery, and the afternoon light was long on the street, and the key swung against my chest with every step, and I was afraid and clear-eyed and moving forward.

For the first time in a long time, those things felt like the same thing.

~ End of Act 2 ~

ACT 3

CHAPTER 28: THE HUNT

Daniel was waiting at the gallery when I arrived, the lights low, the space around us full of other people's art. He had made tea. He had placed two cups on the edge of his desk with the careful deliberateness of a man who has learned that small gestures of normalcy help when the conversation is not going to be normal.

I told him about the notebook. About the hooks. About the photographs I had taken.

He looked at them on my phone in silence for a long time.

"Sarah," he said finally.

"You know who wrote it?"

"I know who she is. I've been trying to find her for two years." He set the phone down. "Her name is Sarah Chen. She met Lucian at a gallery opening in the city, three years ago. Same pattern. Same language. He told her she was the only person in the room who was actually seeing."

I felt the words land somewhere cold in my chest.

"He said the same thing to me."

"He says it to all of them. It's not an accident ~ it's a script. He finds the specific hunger in a person and he feeds it precisely enough to create dependency. With Sarah it was being seen. With Isabelle March it was being protected." He paused. "With you, I think, it was being believed."

I looked at my tea. The accuracy of it moved through me like something physical.

"Isabelle," I said. "Tell me about her."

Daniel was quiet for a moment. When he spoke, his voice was careful in the way of a person carrying something they cannot set down.

"Isabelle March was a gallery curator. Thirty~one years old. She met Lucian at an opening ~ his foundation had funded the show. By all accounts she was sharp, perceptive, good at her work. Her friends say she started to change about four months in. Quieter. More uncertain. She started second~guessing decisions at work that she would previously have made without hesitation."

"He dismantled her professionally," I said.

"He dismantled her entirely. By the time she tried to leave, she had been so thoroughly persuaded that her judgment was unreliable that she didn't trust her own decision to go." He looked at his hands. "She went to the police. Filed a report alleging stalking, harassment. Lucian's lawyer had a response ready within twenty~four hours ~ a counter~narrative about an unstable ex~partner trying to damage a successful man's reputation. The police looked at him and looked at her and made a choice."

"And then?"

"Three days after the report was filed, Isabelle was dead. The police ruled it suicide. Her friends have spent five years not believing that."

The room was very quiet. I thought about a woman who had seen the wolf and gone to the authorities and found that the authorities looked at the wolf and saw a man.

"How many?" I asked. "Total."

"That I can confirm: six. Lena. Isabelle. Sarah. Three others whose names I have but whose full stories I'm still building." He met my eyes. "Possibly more that I haven't found yet."

Six women. Six women who saw the wolf. Six different outcomes, ranging from escaped to dead, all of them connected by a man who gave keys as symbols and called it trust.

"He's going to come back," I said. "To me. He knows I pulled away. He'll let me sit with the doubt for a while and then he'll come back."

"Yes."

"So I need something before he does. Something real. Something that a detective can use."

Daniel looked at me steadily. "What are you thinking?"

"I'm thinking," I said slowly, "that I need to find Sarah Chen."

CHAPTER 29:

It took four days to find her.

I approached it the way I approached design research: methodically, without forcing conclusions, following the thread wherever it went rather than wherever I expected it to go. I found her Twitter account first ~ dormant for two years, but still there, still public, the record of a woman who had needed to write things down so she could not later be convinced she had imagined them.

I recognized the impulse. I had been doing it for years.

I read every post. I took screenshots of the ones that mattered ~ the early ones, where she wrote about a man who saw her in a way she had never been seen before, and the later ones, where the language shifted almost imperceptibly: he says things and then says he never said them. My friends think I'm being dramatic. Maybe they're right. Maybe I'm the problem.

The last thread before she went silent was dated March of the previous year:

I left. I don't know if I'm brave or stupid. Probably both. He came to my apartment and he was crying and he said I was the only person who had ever really seen him and I almost let him in. I had my hand on the door. And then I heard his voice ~ really heard it, underneath the crying ~ and I understood that the crying was not grief. It was fury. It was the fury of something that has been denied what it believes it owns.

I'm posting this so I can't forget. So if I go back, there is a record of what I knew.

If you're reading this and it sounds familiar: trust what you heard underneath. That's the real thing. The crying is the performance. What's underneath is what he is.

She had left the posts up deliberately. A message in a bottle, aimed at whoever came next.

I found her sister through Facebook ~ Emily Chen, a suburb an hour outside the city, her profile picture showing two women with the same dark eyes. I sent a careful message. I told her my name and that I thought we might know the same man and that I was not looking to cause harm, only to understand.

Three days of silence. Then a call from an unknown number.

"Is this Maya?"

The voice was careful. Young but careful, in the way of people who have learned that caution is not the same as fear.

"Yes," I said.

"My name is Sarah," she said. "Emily said you mentioned a man. She said you sounded like you were telling the truth."

"I'm trying to."

A pause. Then: "His name is Lucian."

It wasn't a question.

"Yes," I said.

Another pause, longer. I heard her breathe.

"I'll meet you," she said. "But not in the city. Somewhere I choose."

"Of course," I said. "Wherever you feel safe."

The word safe landed between us like something fragile and important.

"I'm not sure I feel safe anywhere," she said. "But some places are better than others. I'll text you the address."

CHAPTER 30:

She was already there when I arrived. Corner table, back to the wall, positioned with the sight lines of someone who has thought about this. She was thinner than her photographs and there were shadows beneath her eyes that the warm light of the coffee shop couldn't quite soften. But she was present. She was looking at me directly, with the specific attention of a person who has learned to read faces quickly and accurately.

I sat across from her. We looked at each other for a moment without speaking.

"You have the key," she said.

I looked down. The leather cord was visible above my collar.

"He gave it to me on the third date," I said. "He called it a symbol."

Something moved through her face. Recognition and something that might have been pain.

"He gave it to me on the second," she said. "He said it meant he was letting me in. That he didn't show people the real thing and I was different." She wrapped both hands around her cup. "I kept it for four months after I left. I slept with it in my hand some nights. I don't know why. I think I was trying to understand what it had actually been."

"What did you decide?"

"That it was a leash," she said. "Dressed up as a gift. The key didn't open the building. The key opened me." She looked at the cord around my neck. "You should take it off."

"I know," I said. "Not yet. I need it to still look like he has me."

Her eyes sharpened. "You're going after him."

"I'm trying to build something a detective can use. Something that doesn't depend on our word alone."

She was quiet for a long moment. She looked at the table. Then she looked up.

"What do you need?"

She talked for two hours. She told me everything ~ the timeline, the specific language he used at each stage, the way the dismantling happened so gradually that she hadn't understood it was happening until she looked back from outside it and saw the shape of what had been done.

"He finds where you're weak," she said. "Not in a cruel way. He's not cruel at first. He's kind. Extraordinarily kind, in precisely the places that hurt. And you think: someone finally sees it. Someone finally understands. And you open up around that kindness and he learns the whole map of you." She looked at her coffee. "And then he uses it."

"My divorce," I said. "The gaslighting. He used my history of being gaslit to gaslight me."

"Yes. With me it was my father's death. He said he understood grief. He said he would protect me from ever feeling that alone again." Her voice was steady. Practiced. The steadiness of someone who has said this enough times that the saying of it no longer costs the same. "He was the loss. Leaving him was the grief."

I thought about that. About the way he had positioned himself as the solution to the wound he was simultaneously creating.

"Isabelle," I said.

Sarah's hands tightened around her cup.

"I didn't know her," she said. "But I found her, after I got out. I needed to know if I was the first. I found her obituary. I found her friends. I found~" She stopped. "She tried to leave him. She went to the police."

"And they didn't believe her."

"They believed him. He had a lawyer there within hours. He had a story. He was calm and well~dressed and plausible and she was ~ by that point she was frightened and shaking and she'd lost weight and her hands didn't stop moving." Sarah looked at me directly. "You know what a woman looks like after four months with someone who has been methodically dismantling her sense of reality. It doesn't look credible. It looks like instability."

"That's the design," I said slowly. "He makes them look exactly like the person no one will believe."

"Yes." Sarah put her cup down. "He told me once ~ he said it like it was a compliment ~ that he could see the exact shape of a person's self~doubt. That it was like a topographical map. He said most people never learned to read it but he always could."

The coldness in my chest had become something almost solid.

"He said that to you."

"He thought it made him sound perceptive. I think he forgot, by that point, that he was supposed to be pretending." She looked at her hands. "Or maybe he didn't forget. Maybe he was testing how much I'd accept."

We sat for a moment in the particular quiet of two women who have survived the same thing and are comparing maps.

"Will you talk to a detective?" I asked. "Someone I trust. Everything on your terms ~ you choose what you share and when."

She was quiet for a long time. Outside the window, the suburb moved through its ordinary Tuesday afternoon. People walking dogs. A child on a bicycle. A life that had no awareness of what was being discussed in the corner of a coffee shop.

"If you get something real," she said finally. "If you get something that means it won't just be our word against his. Then yes. I'll talk."

I nodded. I reached across the table, not quite touching her hand.

"You left him a message," I said. "In the notebook. You left it for whoever came next."

She looked up. Something moved through her face that I didn't have a name for ~ not quite grief, not quite relief. Something between them.

"I didn't know if anyone would find it," she said. "I didn't know if it would matter."

"It mattered," I said. "It was the first thing that made me certain I wasn't crazy."

She nodded. She looked out the window.

"Good," she said. "Then I'll do the same for the next one. Whatever you build ~ whatever evidence you get ~ we leave it somewhere. So the next woman knows she's not the first. So she knows someone got out."

I thought about Lena's notebook. The single word on the last page.

Run.

I thought about what it would have meant to Lena, at eighteen, to know that someone had survived this and left a map.

"We will," I said. "I promise."

CHAPTER 31:

Detective Reeves had a face that had made its peace with being underestimated. She was perhaps fifty, small, with the particular stillness of someone who has learned that watching is more useful than moving. Her office was neat in the way of someone who has learned that disorder is used against you ~ no personal photographs, no clutter, nothing that could be pointed to as evidence of a mind that didn't have its house in order.

I laid everything on her desk. The photographs from the warehouse. The notebook pages. Sarah's Twitter posts. Daniel's fifteen year file. The recordings I had made of Lucian's texts ~ the full manipulation sequence after the warehouse sighting, each message building on the last.

Reeves looked through it in silence. She read carefully. She did not rush.

When she finished, she set everything in a neat pile and folded her hands on top of it.

"Tell me about the warehouse sighting," she said. "The woman you saw with him."

I told her. The woman's fear. Lucian's empty face. The mask returning.

"Could you identify her?"

"No. I only saw her from behind, and briefly."

Reeves nodded. "The notebook is compelling. The pattern across multiple women is compelling. The text messages are ~ interesting. His use of your history as a gaslighting tool is documented here, which is useful." She paused. "But what I need, to move forward, is something that connects him directly to a crime. Not a pattern of emotional abuse ~ as real as that is, it is extraordinarily difficult to prosecute. I need something physical. Something that ties him to Isabelle March's death, or to a specific criminal act involving one of the other women."

"He has a note," I said. "He told me. He said Isabelle left a suicide note and that he'd kept it. He called it a reminder."

Reeves's expression didn't change, but something shifted behind her eyes. "He told you he kept the note."

"Yes."

"When?"

"We haven't had that conversation yet," I said. "But I think we're going to."

She looked at me for a long moment. "What are you planning?"

I met her eyes. "I'm planning to let him think he's already won."

Another long look. She was reading me the way I was learning to read people ~ looking for the thing underneath, the thing that told the truth before the words did.

"I need you to understand something," she said finally. "If you do this ~ if you go back to him ~ you will be in genuine danger. He is not a man who accepts the loss of something he has decided is his. If he suspects what you're doing~"

"He'll have already decided I'm too afraid to move against him," I said. "He's been operating on that assumption for a long time. He thinks the fear he creates is the same thing as safety."

"And you think it isn't."

"I think," I said, "that the fear is exactly what I'm going to use."

Reeves was quiet for a moment. She looked at the pile of evidence on her desk.

"I'm going to do something I don't normally do," she said. "I'm going to tell you what I need, specifically, and I'm going to trust you to get it without doing anything that gets you killed." She met my eyes. "Don't make me regret that."

"I won't," I said.

She told me what she needed. I listened carefully. I did not write anything down, because I had learned by now not to write things down in places Lucian might find them.

I carried it in my head instead, the way I had learned to carry things that mattered: carefully, without rushing, with both hands.

CHAPTER 32:

I waited three days before I contacted him.

Three days of silence, which I knew he was tracking. He would be watching the gap the way a doctor watches a vital sign ~ measuring what it meant, calibrating his response. A man like Lucian did not experience the absence of contact as relief. He experienced it as information.

I used the three days well.

I had the cameras installed on the first day. Three of them, small and wireless, positioned with care: one in the bookshelf facing the room, one above the kitchen doorway, one angled from the light fitting above my front door. I tested them until the angles were right, until there was no corner of my main room that wasn't covered. I set up the cloud stream and gave Reeves the access link.

I tested the audio from every position in the room. I noted the places where background noise would be a problem and moved a lamp to create a reason to stand in the better positions.

On the second day I called Mel.

She answered on the first ring. "Maya. I've been~"

"I know. I've been thinking." I kept my voice neutral. Not cold, not warm. Thinking. "I owe you a conversation. Can we talk?"

She came over that afternoon. She sat on my couch with her hands in her lap and she looked at me with the careful attention of someone who is trying to read a situation they no longer fully understand. I told her I had been to the warehouse. I told her about the notebook, in general terms. I watched her face.

She was good. She was very good. Her concern looked real because some of it was real ~ I had to keep reminding myself of this, that the love and the possession had always coexisted in her, that the warmth was genuine even if what it was protecting was not.

"What are you going to do?" she asked.

"I'm going to go to him," I said. "I'm going to let him think I've come back."

Something moved through her eyes. I watched it carefully. It was fast ~ there and gone ~ but I had been learning to read things that moved quickly.

It was not fear for me.

It was calculation.

"That's dangerous," she said.

"I know."

"He'll~"

"I know what he'll do. I'm prepared for it." I looked at her steadily. "I need to do this, Mel. You know I need to do this."

She looked at me for a long moment. Then she nodded, slow and deliberate.

"I know," she said. "I've always known I couldn't stop you."

She said it like surrender. I let her believe it was working.

On the third day, I texted Lucian.

Maya: I've been thinking about what you said. About running from things. About letting fear make the decisions.

I waited. Seven minutes.

Lucian: I've been thinking about you.

Maya: I don't want to run anymore.

Lucian: Then don't. Come to me. Let me show you something.

Maya: The warehouse?

Lucian: Not yet. Somewhere that's mine. Really mine. Come tonight.

He sent an address. His apartment. The condominium in the financial district ~ I had found it in public records weeks ago, noted it, filed it.

He wanted me on his territory. Of course he did. A man like Lucian understood the geometry of power: he was always most comfortable when he controlled the room.

I texted Reeves: Tonight. His apartment. I'll call when I'm inside.

Her response: Cameras on. I'm watching. You have thirty minutes before I send someone in.

I looked at the cameras in my apartment. The steady red lights. The cloud stream, open and recording.

I picked up Lena's notebook from my nightstand. I held it for a moment ~ the cloth cover, the worn edges, the weight of fifteen years. I opened it to the last page and I looked at the word she had pressed so hard into the paper it had nearly torn through.

Run.

"Not this time," I said, to the empty room, to Lena, to the eighteen~year~old version of myself who had stood in this gallery and felt the cold and not yet known what it meant.

I put on my coat. I went to meet the wolf.

~ End of Act 3 ~

ACT 4

CHAPTER 33: THE PREY FIGHTS BACK

The lobby was the kind of immaculate that costs money to maintain and more money to make look effortless. Marble floors, cool and pale as bone beneath my feet. Orchids on every surface ~ white, deliberate, their scent faintly medicinal underneath the sweetness, the smell of something cultivated to within an inch of its life. A doorman in dark wool who looked at me the way people in lobbies like this look at women who arrive alone at night ~ assessing, filing, deciding. He called up before letting me through. I stood and waited and listened to the sound of my own breathing and the distant murmur of the city outside the glass and I made myself stay still.

The elevator was mirrored. I watched myself in it ~ coat, jaw, the key no longer around my neck, the absence of it feeling strange against my collarbone, like a tooth pulled. I watched the numbers climb. Twelve. Thirteen. Fourteen. And I ran through the list one more time, the way you run your hand along a wall in the dark ~ not because you doubt it's there, but because the touching is the reassurance.

Cameras rolling at my apartment. Reeves watching. Phone in my pocket, voice memo running. Thirty minutes before she sent someone.

The elevator opened onto a private hallway. Hushed. The carpet thick enough to swallow sound entirely. One door at the end, dark wood, no number.

It opened before I knocked.

Lucian stood in the doorway in a dark sweater, sleeves pushed to his elbows, hair slightly undone. He had calibrated the appearance carefully: the softness of a man at home, the studied dishevelment of someone who was letting you see him unguarded. It was the most controlled version of unguarded I had ever seen.

"Maya." He said my name like relief. Like someone exhaling after holding their breath for a long time. "You came."

"You said you wanted to show me something."

He stepped back.

He let me in.

The apartment was beautiful in the way of a stage set: everything chosen, nothing accidental. Floor~to~ceiling windows, the city spread below like something he had arranged. Art on the walls ~ originals, the kind that didn't announce their price because the price was beside the point. One painting caught my eye: a woman's face in profile, half in shadow, her expression caught between hope and fear.

I recognized the style. I had seen it on the photographs in Daniel's file.

"You collect the artists you know," I said.

"I collect what moves me." He gestured to the couch. "Sit. Please."

I sat. I positioned myself where the angle was best ~ close to the window, my face in the light, nothing behind me that would create shadows. I had thought about this the way I thought about design: light sources, angles, what the eye went to first.

On the coffee table between us, a single object. The key. The one I had returned to him, left on my doorstep after the warehouse, after I decided I needed him to believe I was done.

He had retrieved it. He had placed it here. He wanted me to see that he had it.

"You gave this back," he said, picking it up. "That hurt me, Maya. More than you know."

"I needed to think."

"I gave you space." He turned the key in his fingers. "And now you're here."

"Now I'm here."

He looked at me with the warmth fully deployed ~ the eyes almost, almost smiling, the attention like a physical thing. I had spent weeks feeling what this felt like. I let myself feel it now without flinching, without retreating. I needed to be close enough to the fire to see clearly.

"Why did you come back?" he asked.

"Because you were right," I said. "About running. I've been running my whole life. From Lena's death. From what I saw in that gallery fifteen years ago. From this."

His eyes sharpened. Just slightly. "What did you see in the gallery fifteen years ago?"

"I saw you," I said. "I didn't know it then. But I've been going back through everything and I know now. You were there. You were watching Lena. And you were watching me."

The silence that followed was a particular kind. Not the silence of a man who has been surprised. The silence of a man who has been waiting for something to arrive and is now deciding what to do with it.

"You've been doing your research," he said.

"I've been trying to understand what I saw."

"And what did you see?"

I looked at him steadily. "A man who was deciding something. About Lena. And about me."

He set the key down on the table between us. He leaned back, and something shifted in the room ~ the warmth recalibrating, the performance adjusting for a different audience than the one he had prepared for.

"You're not here because you stopped running," he said. Not cruelly. Assessingly. "You're here because you've found enough to want more."

"Yes," I said.

"And you think I'll give it to you."

"I think you want someone to know," I said. "I think you've always wanted someone to know. You've been leaving traces for fifteen years. The keys. The wall. The notebook you let Sarah leave. You could have removed that notebook at any time. You didn't."

Something moved through his face. I had been watching his face for weeks, learning its vocabulary. This was something I hadn't seen before. Not the mask, not the coldness. Something almost real.

"You think I left it on purpose," he said.

"I think part of you did."

He stood. He walked to the window. He stood with his back to me and looked at the city below.

"You're the first person to say that," he said.

"I know. Because I'm the first person who came back."

CHAPTER 34:

He talked for twenty minutes.

I had expected maneuvering. I had expected more manipulation, more of the patient, reasonable reframing he was so skilled at. I had not expected this: a man standing at a window above a city he had built himself into, talking.

Not confessing. He would not have called it confession. He would have called it finally being understood.

That distinction mattered. I noted it. The voice memo was running.

He talked about Lena first. He talked about her the way you talk about a mistake you have made peace with ~ not with guilt, but with the detachment of someone who has processed an event into a lesson.

"She was frightened," he said. "That was her problem. She saw something real in me and she couldn't hold it. She went small when I needed her to be large." He turned slightly. "I don't say that without compassion. She was eighteen. I was asking something of her that required a kind of courage she hadn't developed yet."

I sat with my hands in my lap and I did not say: you were asking her to disappear into you and call it love.

I said: "What happened to her?"

He was quiet for a moment.

"She tried to leave," he said. "She told a friend ~ not you, someone else ~ that she was frightened of me. The friend told someone else. It became something it didn't need to become." He paused. "I handled it badly. I was younger then. Less patient."

I let the implication of handled it settle into the room without touching it.

"And Isabelle?" I said.

He turned from the window. His face was calm, but there was something underneath the calm now ~ something that had decided to stop hiding, the way the cold had stopped hiding in his face outside the warehouse.

"You know about Isabelle."

"I know she went to the police. I know the police didn't help her. I know she died three days later."

He walked back to the couch. He sat. He looked at me across the table with the key between us and he said, in a voice that was almost gentle:

"Isabelle tried to destroy me. She went to the authorities with a story designed to take apart everything I had built. She was going to take my foundation work. My reputation. My ability to operate." He folded his hands. "I couldn't allow that."

The room was very quiet.

"What did you do?" I asked.

"I went to her apartment," he said. "She let me in. She was ~ she wanted to be talked down. She wanted me to give her a reason to stop. To tell her she was wrong about me." He looked at his hands. "I gave her something else instead. Something that would let her rest."

I looked at him. "The pills."

"She had them already. She'd been struggling. The depression, the anxiety.. whatever you may think. I simply... helped it reach its conclusion."

"And the note."

"She couldn't have written a note by then. So I wrote it for her." He met my eyes. "I know how that sounds. But she was in pain, Maya. Real pain. I ended it cleanly. That's not cruelty. That's a kind of mercy."

The mercy of a man who had decided what was allowed to exist and what was not.

I sat with my hands still in my lap. I did not shake. I had prepared myself for this ~ not for the specific words, but for the specific feeling: the vertigo of hearing something true spoken as though it were ordinary.

"The note is still in your safe," I said.

Something sharpened in his eyes. "How do you know about my safe?"

"Because you told me you kept it. You said it was a reminder."

A pause. He was recalculating. I watched him do it.

"What do you want, Maya?" he said. "Why are you really here?"

"I told you. I'm done running. I want to understand."

"You understand now."

"I want to understand why you let Sarah leave her notebook there. Why you gave the women keys. Why you keep the trophies. What it is you actually want from all of this."

He looked at me for a long time. The warmth was entirely gone now. What was left was the thing I had seen outside the warehouse: the face of a man who had stopped performing because he believed no one was watching.

"I want," he said slowly, “something real with someone..” He looked at the key on the table. "Every woman I've ever been with ~ I have given them the same opportunity. The key. The access. The invitation to see what's really there."

"And when they tried to leave?"

"They chose not to see. They got close to the real thing and they flinched." His voice was flat. Factual. "That's not my failure."

"It's theirs."

"It's a fundamental incompatibility."

I looked at him. I thought about Isabelle, at twenty-five, trying to leave a man who had spent months making her unable to trust herself, going to the police with shaking hands, being disbelieved. I thought about Sarah, locking her door at two in the morning, her sister's headlights in the parking lot. I thought about Lena, eighteen years old, pressing a single word so hard into the back of a notebook it nearly tore through.

I thought about all of them and I sat very still and I said:

"They saw you clearly. That's exactly why they left."

He stood. The movement was fast enough that I pressed back into the couch before I could stop myself. He saw the flinch. He noted it.

"You've been recording this," he said.

My blood went cold.

"Your phone. You've had it running since you sat down." He held out his hand. "Give it to me."

I didn't move.

"Maya." His voice was patient. Patient and absolutely without warmth. “Give me the phone.”

I reached into my pocket. I handed him the phone.

He looked at the screen. He saw the voice memo running. He pressed stop. He held the phone over the table and he dropped it.

The screen cracked. The case split.

"There," he said. "Now we can have a real conversation."

He sat back down. He looked at me across the table. His face was entirely still.

"You're going to go home," he said. "You're going to take whatever you think you have and you're going to let it go." He tilted his head. "This is not the first time someone has tried, Maya. Are you familiar with the outcome? I'll just say you're unstable and I ended things with you. You just couldn't let go."

I looked at him. I thought about the cameras in my apartment. The cloud stream, running, Reeves watching on the other end. I thought about everything I had prepared for this exact moment ~ the thing he didn't know, the second trap inside the trap he thought he'd found.

I thought about what it meant to be a woman who had spent years learning to hide what she knew.

"I'm familiar with the outcome," I said.

"Good." He stood. He walked to the door and opened it. The gesture of a man who has decided the meeting is over. "I'd like you to leave now. I think we both know this was the last time."

I stood. I walked to the door. I stopped in the threshold.

"Lucian," I said.

He looked at me.

"I came here with cameras already running. Not on my phone. In my apartment. Everything you said to me here tonight has been streaming to a server since before my arrival." I held his gaze. "You told me Isabelle couldn't write her own note. You told me you helped her death reach its conclusion. You told me you wrote the note yourself." I paused. "Detective Reeves has been watching for the last forty minutes. She has everything."

Something happened in his face that I had never seen before. Not the mask. Not the coldness. Not the warmth.

The actual thing underneath.

It was much smaller than I expected. And much more frightened.

"You should answer your phone," I said. "When it rings."

I walked out. I did not look back.

In the elevator, going down, I stood very still with my hands at my sides and I waited to feel something. The fear had not come yet ~ my body was still in the state of controlled stillness I had held for forty minutes, the stillness of a woman who knew that the wolf was watching and could not afford to flinch.

The elevator doors opened. I walked through the lobby. The doorman nodded. The night air hit my face.

My phone buzzed. Reeves.

Reeves: We have it. All of it. Stay where you are. Officers are ninety seconds out.

I stood on the sidewalk outside Lucian Voss's building and I looked up at the lit windows of the fourteenth floor and I breathed.

In. Slowly. One. Two. Three. Out slowly.

The fear arrived then, now that it was allowed. It moved through me in a wave ~ my hands shaking, my knees unsteady, the full weight of what had just happened landing all at once. I let it come. I had learned, finally, to let the body say what it needed to say.

I had been afraid. I was still afraid.

And I had not run.

Those two things had always felt like they should be opposites. Standing on a sidewalk in the dark with my hands shaking, I understood for the first time that they were not.

CHAPTER 35:

They arrested Lucian Voss at 11:47 PM. Reeves called me while I was still standing on the sidewalk to tell me. She used the word arrested in the flat, precise way of someone who has been working toward a specific outcome for a long time and is not yet ready to call it done.

"There's more to do," she said. "Corroborating evidence. The note from the safe, if we can get it. Isabelle's friends' statements. But we have the recording. We have the confession. We have Sarah." A pause. "You did well, Maya."

I thanked her. I walked home through the quiet streets. I thought about calling Mel.

I didn't.

I had been thinking about Mel with a particular, careful quality of attention for three days. I had been holding the things I knew and the things I suspected and the things I could not yet make into a complete shape, and I had been holding them gently, the way you hold something that might break or might be exactly as solid as it looks, and you haven't yet decided which.

The text message she had received. She'd been sitting in her car outside my apartment on the night Lucian was arrested, and as she drove away I had watched her on the camera feed ~ watched her stop in the hallway, take out her phone, read something, smile the small private smile of a woman receiving information she had been waiting for.

I had not told her Lucian was coming to my apartment that night.

I had not told her where I was going.

The question that sat underneath all of this, the one I had been circling for days, was not: did Mel know about Lucian. I was almost certain she did.

The question was: what did knowing mean, for a woman who had loved me for fifteen years and confused that love with ownership for just as long?

She called the next morning. Her voice was careful, the way it got when she was working out what I knew before deciding what to tell me.

"I heard," she said. "About Lucian. The arrest." A pause. "Are you okay?"

"I'm okay," I said. "Can you come over?"

She came within the hour. She sat on my couch with a coffee she didn't drink and she looked at me with the focused attention I had known for years, the attention that had always made me feel seen and that I now understood was also an instrument ~ a way of reading the room, of tracking what I knew and what I was going to do with it.

I had thought about how to do this. I had thought about it all night.

I put my phone on the coffee table between us. I opened the camera app. I showed her the saved footage from three nights ago: the hallway, the moment she had stopped, the phone, the smile.

She looked at it. She looked at me.

"Who texted you that night?" I asked.

The silence went on for a long time. I had learned, from Lucian of all people, how to sit in a silence and not fill it.

"He did," she said finally. "Lucian."

"You had his number."

"Yes."

"Since when?"

She closed her eyes. She opened them. She looked at me with an expression I had never seen on her face ~ not the warmth, not the focused attention, not the care. Something underneath all of that. Something exhausted.

"Since Lena," she said.

She talked for a long time. I listened without interrupting.

She had seen Lucian the night Lena disappeared. She had recognized what he was ~ she had, she said, always been good at recognizing that quality in people, the quality of someone who collected and consumed ~ and she had left. She had left and Lena had not, and she had carried the weight of that decision for fifteen years the way a person carries something that has grown into their bones.

She had not told me because she did not want me to look. She did not want me to look because she was afraid of what looking would cost me, and also, underneath that, because she was afraid of what it would cost her ~ the looking, the finding, the moment when I would no longer need her to be the person who held things together.

When Daniel had come to her, four years after Lena disappeared, she had told him what she'd seen. She had given him the information and asked him not to tell me. He had kept that agreement until I came back to town and gave him a reason to break it.

She had known Lucian was in the city. She had known he had found me at the gallery. She had watched it happen ~ watched me come home from that first date flushed and frightened and unable to name why ~ and she had told me to give it a chance. Give it a chance, Maya. Don't let your past ruin something that might be good.

"Why?" I said, when she stopped talking. It was the only question I had.

She looked at her hands. "Because if he broke you," she said, "you would come back to me. The way you always came back to me. And I would be the one who put you back together. The way I always was."

She said it simply. Without drama. Without asking for absolution. The most honest thing she had ever said to me in fifteen years.

I sat with it.

I thought about my mother's advice, which was: “when someone shows you something true about themselves, believe them. Don't revise it into something easier. Believe them.”

"You let him have access to me," I said. "You told him things. Things I told you."

"Not everything. Not~" She stopped. "Some things. Enough that he knew where you were weak."

The map. He had talked about the topographical map of a person's self~doubt. He had told Sarah he could always read it. And I had handed him mine, through Mel, before he ever walked into a gallery and said: you're the only person in this room who's actually seeing.

"Mel," I said.

She looked at me.

"I love you," I said. "I have loved you for years. That is true and it is not going to stop being true."

Her eyes filled.

"And I can't trust you right now. I can't be around you right now. And I need you to understand that both of those things are also true."

She nodded. One small, precise movement.

"Are you going to~" she started.

"I'm going to tell Reeves what you've told me," I said. "That's not negotiable. What she does with it is not my decision."

She nodded again.

She stood up. She looked around the apartment ~ at the photographs on the walls, the books, the small artifacts of a life I was still building. She looked at everything with the expression of a woman taking inventory of something she is leaving.

"I'm sorry," she said. "I know that doesn't~"

"I know you are," I said. "That's what makes it so hard."

She left. The door closed. The lock turned.

I sat in the quiet of the apartment for a long time.

I thought about the ways we are damaged by people who love us badly. How much worse it sometimes feels than being damaged by people who don't love us at all ~ because at least then the wound makes sense. At least then there is no part of you that has to hold the tenderness alongside the harm, has to say: I know why you did it, and I know it cost you something, and I am still sitting here in the rubble of what it cost me.

I opened my journal. I wrote:

She loved me and she held on too tight and the holding damaged things that can't be undamaged. Both of those things are true at the same time. I'm learning to hold two true things at once without needing one of them to cancel the other out.

I closed the journal. I sat with it in my lap.

Outside, the town went about its ordinary morning.

Inside, something was ending. Something else, not yet named, was trying to begin.

CHAPTER 36:

The week after the arrest, I slept for eleven hours a night and woke up tired.

I had not expected that. I had expected relief ~ the clean, expansive relief of a thing finally finished, a door finally closed. I had expected to feel the way the end of a long illness is supposed to feel: weak but clarified, emptied out and ready to be refilled with something better.

Instead I felt nothing in particular. A wide, flat nothing, like a field after a fire. Everything that had been growing there ~ the fear, the purpose, the focused forward motion of a woman with a task ~ was gone. What was left was just ground. Just me, standing in it, not sure what came next.

My therapist, when I called her, said: this is normal. She said it the way she said most things ~ with the calm of someone who has seen the full range of human experience and has made peace with its patterns. She said: "you have been operating in a state of sustained threat response for months. Possibly years, if we count the marriage. Your nervous system doesn't know it's over yet. It will take time to learn."

I said: "how much time."

She said: "as much as it needs."

I said: "that's not an answer."

She said: "I know. I'm sorry. It's the only honest one."

I sat with that for a while after I hung up. The only honest one. I had been surrounded, for so long, by answers that were something other than honest ~ answers that were performances, or management, or the careful construction of a truth incomplete enough to function. I had forgotten what it felt like when someone simply said: I don't know. I'm sorry. That's all there is.

It felt, uncomfortably, like the most intimate thing anyone had said to me in months.

I ate cereal for dinner three nights in a row. Not because I couldn't cook ~ because the sequence of decisions required to produce a meal felt, in those first days, like an unreasonable demand. What do I want. What do I have. What combines with what. The ordinary mathematics of feeding yourself, which I had performed without thinking for thirty-four years, had temporarily exceeded my processing capacity.

I noted this without judgment. My therapist had taught me to do that ~ to observe what was happening in my body and my behavior without immediately converting it into evidence of failure. You are eating cereal for dinner, I told myself. This is what a person does when their nervous system is recalibrating. This is allowed.

I ate the cereal. I watched television I couldn't follow. I went to bed at nine and lay awake until two and slept until noon and woke feeling like I had been somewhere very far away.

On the second night, somewhere between the cereal and the television I couldn't follow, a memory surfaced. Small. Specific. The kind of memory that arrives in the aftermath of things, when the noise has stopped and the quiet is loud enough that the things you filed without examining finally come forward.

Three years ago. Before the divorce, before Mark's particular erosion had reached its furthest point. I had been working on a project ~ a rebrand for a small nonprofit, something I cared about, something that had the potential to become more significant work if it went well. I had told Mel about it over dinner. I had been excited ~ genuinely, visibly excited, the kind of excited I hadn't allowed myself in months because excitement required hope and hope had become expensive.

Mel had listened. She had asked questions ~ the right questions, the ones that showed she was paying attention. And then, at the end, she had said: just be careful not to get too invested. These things fall through. I'd hate to see you disappointed again.

I had deflated. I had told myself she was being realistic. I had told myself it was care ~ she was protecting me from disappointment, the way she had always protected me from things, because that was what Mel did, that was who she was.

The project had fallen through. Not because of anything I did. The funding changed. It happened. And Mel had held me through the disappointment with exactly the warmth and steadiness I had come to depend on.

I had never thought about the sequence of those two things. The deflation first. The disappointment after. The comfort waiting, ready, for the moment it was needed.

I thought about it now.

I thought about how many times, over fifteen years, that sequence had occurred. The gentle redirect before the thing. The steady presence after. The way I had always arrived back at Mel, one way or another, diminished by something and grateful for the hand that steadied me.

I thought: that is either love or architecture.

I thought: I don't know which yet. I am trying to be fair.

I ate my cereal. I turned off the television. I went to bed.

I did not write it in my journal yet. Some things needed to sit longer before they were ready to be named.

On the fourth day, Reeves called.

She was methodical and thorough, which I had come to understand was her version of kindness. She told me where things stood: the recording was being processed, the note from Lucian's safe had been retrieved and sent for handwriting analysis, Daniel's fifteen-year file was being formally reviewed. Sarah had given her statement. Two of the other women had been contacted and were considering doing the same.

"It will take time," Reeves said. "Trials take time. I want you to be prepared for that."

"I know."

"And his lawyer is already~"

"I know," I said again.

A pause. Then, in a slightly different register ~ still professional, but with something underneath it: "How are you doing?"

I looked at the bowl of cereal on my coffee table. At the television I had left on without the sound. At the cameras I had not yet taken down, their small red lights steady in the corners of the room.

"I don't know yet," I said.

"That's the right answer," she said. "For right now, that's exactly the right answer."

I almost left it there. Then I said: "Reeves. He confessed to Isabelle. He confessed to the pattern, the methodology, the note. He talked about Lena ~ about her being frightened, about handling it badly." I paused. "But he never actually said what he did to her. He never accounted for her specifically."

A silence on the line. The silence of a woman who has noticed the same thing and has been waiting to see if I would raise it.

"No," she said. "He didn't."

"Is that ~ is that something you're looking at."

"It's something I'm aware of." Her voice was careful. Precise. "Maya. The confession gives us a great deal. It doesn't give us everything. There are aspects of this investigation that are not finished." A pause. "I want you to sit with that carefully. Not to pursue anything independently. But to understand that Lucian Voss in custody is not the same as all of the answers being in the room."

I sat with that for a long time after we hung up.

Lucian in custody. The recording, the note, the pattern, the confession.

And Lena ~ eighteen years old, bracelet tucked inside her socks, one word pressed so hard into the back of a notebook it nearly tore through ~ still not fully accounted for. Still, in some essential way, not yet found.

I had thought, when I walked out of his apartment building and stood on the sidewalk with my hands shaking and Reeves texting we have it, all of it, that I had done what I came here to do. That the shape of Lena's disappearance had been given its outline at last.

But an outline is not the whole shape. And I had learned, from months of looking carefully at things most people looked away from, that the details left out of a confession were sometimes more significant than the details included.

What had Lucian not said.

What had he not needed to say, because someone else had handled that part.

I did not let myself follow the thought to its conclusion. I was not ready. The ground was still too new, too bare, the field after the fire still smoldering in places.

But I wrote it in my journal that night. Small. Careful. In the handwriting of a woman who has learned to document the things she is not yet ready to examine.

He didn't confess to Lena. Specifically. He talked around her. Reeves noticed. I noticed.

Someone else was in that gallery. Someone who knew where Lena was standing and which hand he used and which doorway they were near.

I am trying to be fair. I am trying to be careful.

I am writing this down so it cannot be taken from me later.

I took the cameras down on the fifth day.

It took longer than it should have. I stood on a chair in the living room with the first one in my hand ~ the one from the bookshelf, the one that had caught Lucian's face as he confessed to a woman he believed was powerless ~ and I held it for a while before I put it in the box.

It had saved me. These small, careful, wired things. I had planned for the plan to fail ~ had assumed the phone would be taken, had built the second layer before the first layer was tested. I had, for perhaps the first time in my adult life, trusted myself enough to prepare for my own instincts being correct.

I put the camera in the box. I got down from the chair.

I sat on the floor of my living room for a while, the box beside me, and I tried to locate the feeling that was supposed to come with moments like this. The triumph. The earned satisfaction of a plan that had worked.

What I found instead was something quieter. Something that didn't have a name yet.

It was in the neighborhood of: I am still here.

Not I won. Not it's over. Just the bare, unadorned fact of continuing to exist in a body that had been afraid for a very long time and was only now, in the strange silence of aftermath, beginning to take stock of what that had cost it.

And underneath that, quieter still, something I was not yet ready to say out loud:

It is not over.

On the sixth day I tried to work.

I sat at my desk with the Yeast of Burden logo file open ~ they had finally settled on a direction, a hand-lettered script with a grain motif that managed to be both artisanal and slightly ominous, which was exactly what they'd asked for ~ and I looked at it for forty minutes without doing anything to it.

My mind kept sliding. Not to Lucian, not to the trial, not to the things I still had to do. To smaller things. To the specific weight of Lena's notebook in my hands the first time I opened it. To Sarah's face in the coffee shop, the way her shoulders had dropped when I said: you're not the first. To Mel's face when she told me the truth, finally ~ the exhausted face of a woman who has been carrying something very heavy and has just set it down.

The truth she told me. And the truth she didn't.

I thought about Mel a lot that week. More than I thought about Lucian.

Lucian was comprehensible, in the end. He was a man who had learned to hunt and had hunted for a long time and had eventually been caught. The arc of that was legible.

Painful, and not finished, and full of women who had deserved better ~ but legible.

Mel was harder.

Because the love had been real. That was the thing I kept returning to, the thing I couldn't resolve into something clean and dismissible. She had loved me genuinely and badly at the same time, in the way that people love when they have never learned to love without holding on.

But I had been sitting for five days in the quiet aftermath of everything, and in that quiet the memory of the nonprofit project had not gone away. It had been joined by others ~ small things, individually insignificant, that were accumulating into a shape I was not yet ready to name.

The time she had suggested a weekend away the month I had started asking questions about Lena's case files at the local library. The way she had described, once, a mutual friend's new boyfriend as the kind of man who finds women who are already broken ~ said lightly, said as observation, but arriving the week after I had told her I was thinking about trying to date again.

The way she had always, always been there. Immediately. Completely. As if she had known, each time, that she would be needed.

I had called it devotion. I had called it the particular grace of a friendship that had survived everything.

I was beginning to understand that presence could be a form of management. That always being there, for fifteen years, required always knowing where there was.

I missed her. That was the most uncomfortable truth of the week. In the grey aftermath of everything, when the adrenaline was gone and the purpose was gone and I was just a woman eating cereal on a couch in a rented house in her hometown, I missed my best friend. I missed her texts. I missed her laugh. I missed the specific way she could make the heaviest things feel temporarily lighter.

I missed her and I was also, I understood now, relieved that she was not here. Because the lightness she had always offered me had come at a cost I was only now beginning to calculate.

And I was beginning to wonder if the cost had been paid by more people than just me.

Later. There would be time, later, to figure out what Mel was to me and what she could be and what the shape of that looked like going forward.

Not yet. Not in the grey zone.

Not until I understood what she had known about Lena. And for how long.

And what she had done with that knowledge.

On the seventh day I went outside.

Not for a reason. Not to go anywhere particular. I put on my coat and my shoes and I opened the front door of the rental house and I stood on the porch in the November cold and I breathed.

The town was doing what small towns do: existing, quietly, in the particular way of places that have been existing for a long time and have made peace with their own continuity. A woman walked a dog past the gate. A car idled at the corner. From somewhere down the street came the sound of someone's radio, an old song, something with a trumpet.

I stood on the porch and I listened to the trumpet and I looked at the ordinary street and I tried to locate myself in it. Maya. Thirty-four years old. Divorced. Returned. Resident, for now, of a rented house with a porch swing that creaked in the wind and a kitchen window that faced south toward a gallery with iron doors.

Still here.

Still here, and the wolf was in custody, and the evidence was being processed, and Sarah was in her suburb getting slightly better every day, and Daniel was continuing to look carefully at things other people looked away from, and Detective Reeves was doing whatever Detective Reeves did when she went home at night, and the young woman who would eventually stand beside me in a gallery and tell me about a feeling she was afraid to trust didn't know yet that any of this had happened.

The world was very large. The street was very ordinary. The trumpet played.

I sat down on the porch swing. It creaked under my weight, that same questioning sound, and I let it move me slightly in the cold air, back and forth, the way it must have moved whoever had sat here before me, whoever had rented this house and sat on this swing and looked at this street.

I thought: I don't know what comes next.

I thought: that's all right. That's allowed.

I thought: I have been so focused on what needed to be done that I have not thought, in a long time, about what I actually want. What I want to build. What kind of life fits the woman I have become, which is a different woman than the one who packed three boxes into a Camry and drove back to a hometown she had been avoiding for fifteen years.

I didn't have answers. I had, for the first time in months, the space to begin asking.

But underneath the asking ~ underneath the cautious, careful beginning of something that might, eventually, become rest ~ one question that would not stay filed. One question that surfaced every time the quiet got loud enough.

What happened to Lena. Specifically. And who else was in the room.

I did not have the answer yet.

I understood, sitting on the swing in the November cold, that I was going to have to find it.

Not today. Today was for breathing and the ordinary continuing world.

But soon.

That felt, cautiously, like something.

That night I cooked. An actual meal ~ pasta, a sauce from scratch, something that required chopping and timing and the small sequential decisions I had not been able to manage a week ago. I stood at the stove and I stirred and I listened to the radio and I ate at the kitchen table with a glass of wine and a book I didn't read.

I sat there for a long time after I finished eating. Just sitting. Not doing anything. Not planning or building or documenting or preparing for the thing that came next.

Just sitting at a kitchen table in a rented house in November, in the specific silence of a woman who has survived something and is only now, in the quiet, beginning to understand the full dimensions of what that means.

It means: she is still here.

It means: the ground beneath her is hers.

It means: whatever comes next, she will walk into it with her eyes open, with her instincts intact, with the knowledge ~ hard-won, expensive, worth every penny of what it cost ~ that the voice that says something is wrong is not a malfunction.

It is the most reliable thing she has.

I took out my journal. I opened it to a blank page.

I wrote:

I don't know what I am yet. On the other side of this. I thought I would feel finished and I feel unfinished, which my therapist says is right, which I am choosing to believe.

I am going to stay in this town a little longer. Not because I have to. Because I want to. Because there is something here I haven't finished yet that has nothing to do with Lucian or Mark.

It has to do with Lena. And possibly with Mel. And with the question I keep not asking because I am not yet sure I am ready for the answer.

Tomorrow I'm going to the cemetery. Not because I have anything resolved to tell her. Just to sit with her for a while. Just to be there.

But after that.

After that I am going to start asking the question I have been circling.

What did Mel know. When did she know it. And what did she do.

I am writing this down so I cannot be convinced, later, that I didn't see it coming.

I saw it coming. I am choosing, for one more day, not to look directly at it.

Tomorrow I will look.

I closed the journal. I washed the dishes. I turned off the kitchen light.

The house settled around me, its old wood making the sounds old wood makes, the sounds of a structure that has been here a long time and intends to continue.

I went to bed. I slept for eight hours.

When I woke up, it was morning.

It was just morning ~ ordinary, grey, and cold ~ but it was mine, and I lay in it for a while before I got up, the way a person does when they are no longer bracing for what the day will require of them.

The way a person does when they have, finally, stopped running.

And started, instead, to rest.

Before the next thing begins.

CHAPTER 37:

Three months after Lucian Voss's arrest, I went back to the cemetery.

The scar on my arm from the cabin ~ from the night I had gone after Mel, the night she had made her own terrible decision in a kitchen with a small paring knife and fifteen years of guilt ~ had faded from red to pink. I touched it sometimes without meaning to, when I was thinking about something difficult. It had become a kind of punctuation mark. A comma in the sentence of what I had survived.

Not a period. A comma.

The grass on Lena's grave had been cut recently. Someone maintained this plot, though I didn't know who. The brass plaque was the same ~ tarnished, the letters worn at the edges ~ but it looked, somehow, less final than it had the day I arrived back in this town.

I knelt. I put my hand flat on the grass.

"I know what happened," I said. "Not everything. Probably not everything ever. But enough. Enough to give it a shape."

The river glittered in the distance. The trees moved.

"The man who hurt you is in custody. There will be a trial. It won't be enough ~ trials are never enough, they don't give back what was taken, they don't un~do the un~doing. But it's something. It's a shape where there was formlessness."

I looked at the plaque. Beloved Daughter. Still only that.

"You tried to tell someone," I said. "You wrote it down and you tried to run and it wasn't enough and that was not your failure. That was a failure of the world you were in. The world that looked at a man like him and saw a man and looked at a woman like you and saw instability."

The wind moved through the grass.

"I'm trying to change that. Slightly. In the ways available to me. I know it's not enough. I know you needed it fifteen years ago and not now." My voice broke, just slightly, for the first time. "I'm sorry it took me this long. I'm sorry I ran. I should have trusted what my body was telling me the night I stood in that gallery and felt his eyes and knew, somewhere below language, that something was wrong."

I sat for a while after that without speaking. Just sitting, the way I had learned to sit with difficult things ~ not demanding resolution, not performing grief, just being present with the weight of it.

When I stood, my knees ached. I brushed the grass from my jeans.

"I'm going to keep going," I said. "I'm going to keep writing things down and leaving marks and telling the women who come after me that the voice is not a malfunction. That the cold at the back of the neck is information. That the body knows before the mind allows it."

I looked at the plaque one last time.

"I'll come back," I said. "When I know more. When there's more to tell."

I walked back to my car. The town was below me, small and particular and mine in some ways and not mine in others. I drove down the hill and through the streets I had been learning to live in again.

I passed the gallery. I didn't look away.

EPILOGUE:

THE ONE WHO SEES

Six months later, I went to a gallery opening.

Not the gallery ~ a different one, smaller, run by two women who had started it in a former auto repair shop and kept the old signage as a kind of joke that had become a kind of identity. The art was strange and specific and occasionally beautiful. The crowd was the usual crowd: people performing the act of looking while mostly being seen.

I had started going to openings again. Not to meet people, not to network, not for any of the reasons I had gone before. I went because art galleries were where I had learned to trust my instincts again, and I was not going to let a man with pale eyes take that from me.

I was standing in front of a large canvas ~ something abstract, all reds and deep browns, something about weather or anger or both ~ when I felt the young woman come to stand beside me.

She was perhaps twenty-four. She had the look of someone who had dressed carefully for tonight and was not sure it was enough. She was holding her wine glass in both hands without drinking from it.

She was looking at the door.

I knew that look. I had worn it myself, in another gallery, on a night that had changed the shape of everything.

I looked across the room. A man was watching her. He was perhaps forty, polished, positioned against a column with his weight distributed in the particular way of someone who occupies space without appearing to try. His eyes were light. Even from here I could see what they were doing.

Cataloging.

He saw me looking. For a moment we looked at each other across the crowded room. He held it for a beat ~ the assessing pause of someone deciding whether I was relevant ~ and then he shifted his attention back to the young woman beside me.

Dismissing me. That was fine. That was exactly what I needed.

I turned to the young woman.

"The piece next door is better," I said. "In the smaller room. Let me show you."

She looked at me. Her face was uncertain ~ the specific uncertainty of a woman who is trying to work out whether to trust an instinct she has been taught is unreliable.

I knew that look too.

"Okay," she said.

We walked into the smaller room. It was less crowded. The art was quieter. I positioned us near the window, in the light, with the door visible and the room open behind us.

She exhaled. Just slightly. Just enough.

"There's a man out there," I said. "He was watching you."

She went still. "I know."

"You felt it."

"I thought I was imagining it."

"You weren't."

She looked at me. Her face was doing several things at once ~ relief and embarrassment and something beneath both of them that I recognized as the particular gratitude of a woman who has been told, for perhaps the first time: your instincts are correct.

"How did you know?" she asked.

"Because I was standing next to you and I felt it too," I said. "And because I've felt it before. And because I've learned ~ it took me a long time to learn, and I'm still learning ~ that the cold feeling at the back of your neck is not a malfunction. It is information. Your body is telling you something true."

She looked at her wine glass. "I always think I'm being dramatic."

"I know. I did too." I looked at the art on the wall ~ a small, careful painting of a woman's hands. "Someone spent years teaching me that the way to be a reasonable, rational person was to override every instinct that made me inconvenient. And it took me a very long time to understand that the instincts were not the problem. The lesson was."

She was quiet for a moment. Outside the window of the smaller room, I could see the main gallery, the crowd, the man against the column now talking to someone else. Already moving on. Already recalibrating.

They always did. That was both the horror of it and the practical vulnerability: they were efficient. Patient. They moved from loss to the next possibility without apparent grief.

But they could be seen. That was what they didn't fully account for: that the women they trained to doubt themselves were also, some of them, learning to see. Were also, some of them, leaving marks. Were also, some of them, standing in the smaller room of a gallery six months after the worst year of their lives and saying to a young woman with both hands on her wine glass: you are not imagining it. Your body is telling you the truth.

"What do I do?" the young woman asked.

"Right now? Stay in this room a little longer. Let him find someone else. And then go home by a route you choose, not one you're steered toward."

"And if I see him again?"

"Trust the feeling," I said. "Not the voice that says you're being dramatic. The other one. The one that's been trying to tell you something since the moment he walked in." I looked at her. "And if you need someone to believe you ~ find someone who has been through something similar. Not because we have all the answers. But because we can tell you: we felt it too. And we were right."

She looked at me for a long time. Her hands had relaxed around her glass. Her shoulders had dropped half an inch.

"How will I know the difference?" she asked. "Between a real alarm and just ~ anxiety? Just being afraid of things?"

It was the right question. It was the question I had been living inside for two years.

"I don't know if there's a clean answer," I said honestly. "But here's what I've found: anxiety is general. It's ambient. It's a static that runs under everything. What I'm talking about is specific. It has an object. It has a direction. It lands."

I touched the scar on my forearm, briefly, without meaning to.

"And when it lands," I said, "you write it down. You write down the time and the place and what you felt and what you saw. Not for anyone else. For yourself. So that later ~ when the reasonable voice starts asking whether you imagined it ~ you have something to go back to. Something in your own handwriting that says: no. I was there. I felt this. It was real."

She nodded slowly.

"Okay," she said. "Okay."

We stood together in the smaller room for a while, looking at the paintings. After a few minutes she said she was going to find her friend. She thanked me. I told her she didn't need to thank me.

She was almost at the door when she turned back.

"What's your name?" she asked.

"Maya," I said.

She smiled. Small and real and new.

"I'm going to remember that," she said.

She walked out into the main gallery. I watched her find her friend ~ a woman her age, easy and laughing ~ and fold herself into that ease. I watched her not look toward the column where the man had been standing.

He was gone. He had moved on. He would go to another gallery, another opening, another woman who was trying to rebuild something and didn't yet know that the particular attention she was receiving had been calibrated for exactly that vulnerability.

I could not stop all of it. I knew that. I had known it since the night Reeves told me about Lucian's arrest and I had thought: he is just one. There are many others. There will always be others.

But the young woman with both hands on her wine glass would carry something out of this gallery that she had not carried in. A small, specific thing: the knowledge that the feeling was real. That someone else had felt it. That the cold at the back of the neck was information, not malfunction.

That was a mark. The kind that could be passed on.

I thought about Lena's notebook. About Sarah's tweets, still up, still findable by whoever came next. About the small, stubborn act of leaving something behind so the next woman would not have to start from nothing.

We leave marks. That was the thing he didn't understand ~ had never understood ~ about the women he hunted. He thought he was the only one who left traces. He thought the keys and the walls and the notebooks were his, his testimony, his control.

He didn't understand that every woman who survived him left something too. A thread, or a word, or a name written in a journal at two in the morning, or a conversation in the smaller room of a gallery. Something that said: I was here. I saw it. I'm telling you so you don't have to find it alone.

I picked up my bag. I walked through the main gallery, past the column where the man had stood, past the bruise-colored paintings and the careful crowds and the clinking glasses.

I walked out into the night.

The air was cold. The street was ordinary. The city moved around me in its usual indifferent way, full of people going about the business of being alive.

I walked home through streets I had learned to know again. Past the pharmacy, the diner, the hardware store. Past the gallery with its iron doors, closed now, the building that had been the center of my fear for fifteen years and was now just a building on a street I walked on.

I touched the scar on my arm. I thought about the young woman's hands relaxing around her glass. I thought about Sarah in her suburb, checking her locks four times, getting a little better every day. I thought about Daniel, who had spent fifteen years looking carefully at something everyone else looked away from.

I thought about Daniel for longer than I meant to.

He had given me the file. He had brought me into this. He had spent fifteen years building a case against Lucian and had never, in all that careful looking, landed on Mel. A woman who had been in the same room as Lena the night she disappeared. A woman Daniel had spoken to, early in his investigation, who had told him just enough to seem cooperative.

I had been telling myself this was grief making him blind. The particular blindness of someone looking so hard at one thing they couldn't see what was beside it.

But Daniel was not a man who missed things. I had watched him work. I had seen the file, the fifteen years of careful, methodical, unflinching attention to detail. He did not miss things.

Which meant either Mel had been invisible to him.

Or she hadn't.

I stood on the pavement outside my rental house and I held that thought for the first time without immediately setting it down. I let it be what it was ~ unresolved, uncomfortable, the shape of a question I did not yet have the answer to but could no longer pretend I wasn't asking.

Daniel. Who had come to Mel and been told just enough. Who had then come to me. Who had given me everything I needed to go after Lucian and had been, throughout, the person who controlled what I saw and in what order.

I thought about wolves. About the ones who announced themselves and the ones who didn't. About the ones you felt before you saw them and the ones who stayed so far inside your peripheral vision that by the time you turned they were already somewhere else, already innocent, already the person who had been trying to help you all along.

I thought: I am tired. I am six months out from the worst year of my life and I am standing on a pavement being afraid of a man who gave me a file and helped me catch a predator.

I thought: and Lena's truth is still incomplete. And Mel knew which hand. And there is a key in a kitchen drawer that I have not been able to stop thinking about since the night I found it.

I thought: I told myself I would look. I told myself, in the grey zone, after the cereal and the cameras and the pasta, that I would look.

Not tonight. Tonight was for the young woman and the smaller room and the ordinary cold street and the fact that I was still here, still walking, still choosing to come home.

But soon.

I walked into my rental house. I turned on the kitchen light. The blind over the window was still down ~ I had stopped lifting it every morning to check the gallery's iron doors. I didn't need to anymore.

I put the kettle on. I sat at the kitchen table. I opened my journal.

Before I wrote anything I sat for a moment with the pen in my hand and I let myself feel the full weight of what I didn't know yet. Not with dread ~ I had learned, finally, to hold difficult things without bracing against them. Just with honesty. The honesty of a woman who has spent a year learning to trust herself and understands that trusting yourself sometimes means acknowledging the questions you haven't finished asking.

Lucian was in custody. The confession was on record. Isabelle's note was in evidence. Sarah was in her suburb. The trial would take time and his lawyer was already working and none of it was clean or finished or enough.

And Lena ~ her bracelet tucked inside her socks, her one word pressed so hard into paper it nearly tore through ~ Lena was still, in some essential way, not yet fully found.

I had promised her I would come back when I knew more.

I knew more. Not everything. Not yet.

But more than I had known when I stood at her grave in October and put my hand flat on the cold ground and said: I'm not pausing anymore.

I was not pausing.

I had a letter to write. To the next woman. Whoever she was, wherever she was, standing in some gallery with her hands tight around a wine glass and a cold feeling at the back of her neck that she was trying very hard to dismiss.

But first ~ one more entry. For myself. In my own handwriting. So it could not be taken from me later.

I wrote:

Lena's truth is not complete. Lucian confessed to the pattern and to Isabelle and to fifteen years of hunting. He talked around Lena. Someone else was in that room. I know who was standing near the second doorway. I know which hand she described.

Daniel spent fifteen years looking and never found Mel. I need to understand why.

I am not ready to say what I think that means. But I am writing it down. Because that is what I do now. I write things down so they cannot be rewritten for me later.

I promised her I would come back.

I'm coming back.

She closed the journal. She set it on the table ~ not under the mattress, not hidden. On the table, in the light, where she could see it.

That was new. That was different from the woman who had arrived in this town four months ago with three boxes and a hollow feeling and the practiced discipline of someone who had learned that some things required working up to.

She had worked up to it. She was ready.

She picked up her pen. She began the letter to the next woman.

She wrote for a long time.

When she finished it was late and the street outside was quiet and the house was settled around her in its old wood way, its sounds the sounds of a place that had been here a long time and intended to continue.

She folded the letter. She put it in her bag.

Tomorrow she would figure out where to leave it. Somewhere findable. Somewhere that the next woman ~ whoever she was, wherever she was coming from, whatever she had been through ~ could find it without having to look too hard.

That was the point. That had always been the point.

You left the marks where they could be found.

You made sure no one had to start from nothing.

She turned off the kitchen light. She went to bed. She slept ~ deeply, without dreaming, the sleep of a woman whose body had finally, cautiously, begun to believe it was safe.

When she woke, it was morning.

An ordinary morning ~ grey and cold and hers.

She lay in it for a while.

Then she got up.

There was still work to do.
And she was, at last, someone who knew how to do it.

~ The End ~

This book deals with difficult things because difficult things happen to real people. If anything in these pages stirred something in you ~ something you've been carrying, something you haven't yet named ~ please know that support exists and that you deserve access to it. You don't have to have the whole shape of it figured out before you ask for help. You just have to reach out.

The rest can come after.

NOTE FROM THE AUTHOR

If you felt seen by this book, that was the intention. If something in Maya's voice sounded familiar ~ the second-guessing, the practiced discipline of someone who has learned to manage themselves, the moment when the instinct finally gets to be right ~ then you already understand why this story needed to exist.

Thank you for reading it.

Thank you for trusting your own cold feeling at the nape of the neck.

It is not a malfunction.

It never was. Listen to it.

Take Care ~ JC

She walked through.

The Wolf, it circles still. Hunger never satisfied

But the path ~ it held.

Remember, Straight.
      Not easy.
            Straight.

She learned to write it down.
She learned to trust the cold.
She learned that being seen and
being safe were never the same thing ~
until she made them so.
Still standing. Still going.

Still Trusting.

Keep going (;)

~ /

www.ingramcontent.com/pod-product-compliance
Lightning Source LLC
LaVergne TN
LVHW010902110826
845149LV00005B/1448

* 9 7 9 8 9 8 8 4 6 4 8 9 1 *